After her husband is killed ███████████, Rosemary Blake scarcely car████ ████ere she goes. For the sake of her two children, she hesitantly agrees to take a long summer holiday in New England, where her elder sister, Celia, is living. At Celia's suggestion, Rosemary exchanges houses with an American family, and so begins a crash course in American culture that includes everything from Welcome Wagon to summer camp to Fourth of July celebrations—not to mention randy Errol, resident tomcat.

But for Rosemary, Tessa and Timothy it is also a crash course in fear. Why is Celia so different, and what is this mysterious 'executive burn-out' that allegedly ails her husband? And why so many fire sirens? As the dry summer wears on and the risk of forest fire becomes a reality, the Blake family, along with their neighbors, are forced to recognize that the fires are not accidental. Someone in this pleasant, normal community is a pyromaniac—a pyromaniac who, if thwarted, is quite prepared to kill. . . .

(continued on back flap)

mas and *The Cruise of a Deathtime*, she serves as secretary of the Crime Writer's Association.

A TRAIL OF ASHES

A TRAIL OF ASHES

Marian Babson

Walker and Company
New York

First published in the United States of America
in 1985 by the Walker Publishing Company, Inc.

Library of Congress Cataloging in Publication Data

Babson, Marian.
  A trail of ashes.

  I. Title.
PS3552.A25T7   1985   813'.54   84-15315

Printed in the United States of America

10   9   8   7   6   5   4   3   2   1

CHAPTER 1

After the first death, there is no other . . .

There's truth in that. Perhaps that was the reason we—the children and I—managed to survive that terrible summer. The strangeness, the overpowering heat, the odd unfamiliar accents, the menace hanging over the alien house, were all part of the unreality that had enveloped us from the first unbelievable moments of that long unending nightmare . . .

It didn't matter if dinner was late, a steak-and-kidney pudding was on the stove and could go on simmering away indefinitely. The new potatoes were scraped and ready to go on the stove as soon as John returned from his dubious errand of mercy. The greens were also ready. We could have a leisurely drink while everything cooked. By the end of the second drink, dinner would be ready.

The children were in the garden playing on the swings. I glanced through the kitchen window in time to see them lifting Esmond on to a swing for the umpteenth time and patiently explaining to him just what was required of him.

The cat had ideas of his own. None of those ideas included auditioning to be 'The Cat on the Flying Trapeze' for the Sideshow at next Saturday's Gymkhana.

As soon as Timothy, with a few final soothing pats, released his grasp and moved behind the swing for a good hearty push, Esmond was off.

He fled across the garden and into the shrubbery with Timothy and Tessa in hysterical pursuit, calling upon him to come back and play the game—for Queen and Country.

I was still laughing when the doorbell rang and I went to answer it.

To this day, that bothers me. How could I have been laughing? Why didn't I know?

The policeman at the door was shocked. He obviously felt I should have known. He frowned down on me with bleak disapproval.

I stopped laughing then. Even before he spoke, I began to know.

'I'm sorry.' Hazel Davies approached me after the funeral. 'I'm so terribly sorry. If it hadn't been for me—'

'Yes,' I said. She had put it into words. It was the truth and I could not bring myself to utter any of the platitudes.

What could I say: *It's all right?* It was not all right. John was dead and it was all wrong. *It wasn't your fault?* She had enough people assuring her of that. And it *was* her fault—although not directly.

She was there—and her husband wasn't. And my husband had always been too obliging for his own good—fatally obliging. He'd see to that little problem with the fuse wire—no trouble at all. A simple job for a do-it-yourselfer. Hadn't he built another room on to our house—electric wiring and all?

No problem. It was the least he could do for a new neighbour whose husband was travelling overseas helping with Britain's constant Export Drive.

The least he could do—the last thing he did. Driving home, he was sideswiped by another driver, forced off the road on the crest of the hill—and killed.

It wasn't directly Hazel's fault—but she was right. If it hadn't been for her, he'd have been at home with me and the children when that other driver—drunk, the police assumed, or well over the limit—had gone careering over the hilltop. The driver would have hit-and-run from some other car, killed someone else's husband. Or perhaps there'd have been no other car there at all. He'd have negotiated the high curve safely and gone home without a crash—a killing—on his conscience. If he had a conscience.

But John had been there at the wrong moment—just one of those things. Except that it was the end of the world for us and I couldn't dismiss it with a philosophical shrug.

'I'm sorry,' Hazel said again. Her eyes filled with tears as she turned away.

I watched her go, unable to answer. The children pressed against me, staring after her with hostile eyes.

She was not without her comforters. I tried not to hold it against those who spoke soothingly to her. Intellectually, I could understand their reaction. Viewed objectively, it was a terrible thing to have happened to a newcomer to the town, to be responsible—even indirectly—for the death of one of its leading young citizens.

People were sorry for her; they were sorry for me. Torn in their loyalties, friends were trying to be fair to both of us. I must not condemn them for it.

'Are you all right?' Someone touched my arm.

Are you all right? Someone or other had been asking me that stupid question ever since it happened. How all right could I be—ever again?

'Are you all right?' My sister had telephoned from the States, but had realized the imbecility of the question, even as she asked it. 'Financially, I mean,' she amended swiftly.

'Oh, that—yes. John has—had—the kind of insurance policy that took care of paying off the mortgage if anything—'

'Shall I come over for the funeral?' Celia had cut in quickly, before the tears had time to flow again. 'It would be awkward, with Patrick not at all well, but I could manage—' She stopped. 'I didn't mean that the way it sounded,' she apologized. 'I'll come, of course, if you want me.'

'No, don't bother,' I said. I didn't want anyone but John. He was gone and no else mattered.

'Are you all right?' The voice beside me was insistent, trying to be kind.

'Yes . . .' *Yes. What do you expect me to say: I'm walking on air? I'm dancing on the ceiling?*

'Yes . . .' I turned to face Lania and Piers. I looked at them bleakly, thinking that Lania had never been renowned for her tact. When a woman has just buried her man, it isn't especially thoughtful to remind her that some women have two. At least, Lania might have come to the funeral with her own husband.

'Richard had to stay in town overnight,' she said, as though reading my mind. 'He asked me to apologize. He had to entertain customers until quite late and then stay over at his club. He had a business conference this morning and didn't know when he'd be able to get away. Otherwise, he would have been here. He wouldn't have missed it—'

She broke off, realizing that she was exaggerating her husband's enthusiasm for seeing my husband off on his final journey. That was the trouble with occasions like this. There was almost nothing anyone could say that didn't sound wrong.

'Yes,' I said. Tessa was beginning to shiver; Timothy was dead white and swallowing hard. I couldn't worry about the insensitivity of the adults surrounding me. The children were my business—they were all I had left of John; all I could do for him. They had to come first.

'Excuse me—' I bared my teeth mechanically at Lania and her lover; perhaps it looked like a smile, perhaps it didn't; it was a barely-remembered social gesture, nothing more. 'I must get the children home. They've had a . . . difficult morning.'

'We'll give you a lift,' Lania said quickly. 'Unless the undertaker is going to. I know you haven't a car any longer—' She broke off abruptly. She had said the wrong thing again.

'You go along,' I said. 'He'll take care of us—it's all part of the service.'

Celia rang again that night. 'What are you going to do now?' she demanded, in her elder-sister-setting-the-world-to-rights way.

'I'm going to bed,' I answered literally. 'I tucked the children in a couple of hours ago. I'm glad the phone didn't wake them.' We all ought to be asleep by now; it was a good day to have over.

'Not *now* . . .' She sighed with exasperation. 'I mean, tomorrow, next week, from now on . . . ?'

Tomorrow and tomorrow and tomorrow . . . I hadn't thought that far ahead yet.

'Listen,' she said, correctly interpreting my silence. 'I've had a marvellous idea. Why don't you come over here? Just for the summer . . . just till you get your feet under you again.'

'No!' I couldn't face the thought of leaving the place where we had been happy. 'I'm sorry, Celia,' I tried to soften the outright refusal. 'We couldn't afford it. You don't have enough room to put us up . . .'

'That's the beauty of it,' she said, 'I wouldn't have to. Now, just listen—' She was talking quickly to override my arguments. 'Patrick's cousin, Nancy, is married to a schoolteacher who wants to do some research in England for his Ph.D. thesis. Something dreary about Victorian politics—but that doesn't matter. The point is, they have a summer break from mid-June to the beginning of September when school starts again here, which would be ideal for doing research. They have twins, a boy and a girl, just about the same age as your Timothy and, in the ordinary way, they couldn't afford to go over to England for that length of time—'

'Celia,' I broke in, 'this is all very interesting, but—'

'*And* they have a lovely old house in Cranberry Lane, right by the lake!' she finished triumphantly. 'It's absolutely perfect—you can do a house swap and solve both sets of problems!'

'That won't solve my problem, Celia,' I reminded her. I felt tears begin to gather. Esmond leaped on to the desk and rubbed his warm furry body against my face and arm, sensing that comfort was needed, willing to do all he could. Unfortunately his all wasn't much better than Celia's.

'It won't make it any worse,' Celia said shrewdly. Nothing could make it any worse. 'You needn't worry about Nancy and Arnold being careless with your things, they're very conscientious. And house swapping does work out beautifully—everyone is doing it these days. Remember a couple of years ago, Patrick and I swapped with that nice French-Canadian couple and had a lovely cottage in the Laurencians for three weeks? It couldn't have been better!'

'I'm glad it worked out well for you, Celia,' I said. 'However, I really don't feel I could face any more upheaval. I'm too exhausted—'

'Oh, it wouldn't be right away,' Celia said. 'I'll have to work on—I mean, It couldn't happen until after school gets out here in June. And I haven't even mentioned it to Nancy and Arnold yet.'

'That's another thing,' I said. 'What about the children? If you say schools are closed there all summer, they'll miss out a term.'

'There's a marvellous Summer Camp here at Edgemarsh Lake. It's a boarding camp, but they take a few locals as day pupils. It's almost like a school. They have swimming lessons, woodcraft, painting, wind-surfing—all sorts of arts and crafts. It would do them good. Luke loves it—he could show them the ropes.'

Just for a moment, I wavered. The children undoubtedly would love it—and it might be as good for them as a regular term, and they could make up any work they missed easily enough. But . . .

'I can't, Celia. Honestly I can't. It's all too much. The packing, the chaos, the upheaval—' Esmond chirruped sympathetically and butted my chin with his head. 'The cat!' I clutched at him gratefully. 'We couldn't take Esmond with us and—'

'There's no problem, they've got a cat, too. Don't you see how perfect it is? You'll be walking into houses com-pletely equipped, even down to the cat. It would make the children feel right at home. The Harpers can take care of Esmond and you can take care of Errol. Why not? You know you always planned to come over for a nice long holiday some day—' She broke off, conscious that she had gone too far.

'But not like this—' John and I had talked about it, planning it for some distant time when the children were older and we could have more time together.

'I'm sorry. You know what I meant—'

'I know—' I fought to keep the tears out of my voice. 'Thank you, Celia. It was kind of you to think of it. Perhaps some other year . . .'

'I shouldn't have mentioned it so soon.' She was contrite. 'You need time to get used to the idea. I won't take this as final. Just think it over . . .'

'Yes,' I said, with no intention of doing anything of the sort. 'I'll think it over. Goodbye, Celia.'

The days dragged past; somehow we got through them. Our thoughts circled in the endless loop: *this time last week . . . this time last month . . .* I began to understand why tradition decreed a year of mourning. As the sad anniversaries slipped by, perhaps some of the poignancy would begin to fade. Perhaps twelve months would alleviate the immediacy of the pain. And perhaps not. Meanwhile I felt as though I were swimming underwater through the days.

Everyone was very kind. Lania kept popping round with baked or, being Lania, half-baked offerings. Her cooking was never as good as her intentions. For the time being, she was tactful enough to keep quiet about her own complicated love-life.

There was a letter from Celia, restating all her arguments in favour of a summer in America. I threw the letter away.

Friends included the children on outings, whenever they could be persuaded to go. They accepted few of the invitations they received and the anxious way they rushed back into the house at the end of the day told me the reason why. Insecure and frightened by the sudden loss of one parent, they were terrified that something might have happened to me in their absence, that they might return some evening to find that I, too, had slipped away and they were left alone.

Deep down, I felt the same about them. Although I encouraged them to go out with their friends, I was relieved and thankful when they returned safely from their infrequent expeditions. We clung to each other like shipwrecked castaways, trying to pretend we weren't as bereft as we were, secretly waiting for the next blow to fall.

On several occasions I saw Hazel Davies when we were both out shopping. I couldn't help my reaction, I always crossed the street to avoid speaking to her.

The days marched past, slowly and inexorably. The legal formalities were sorted out. The pain remained. It was nearly the end of term and the children would soon be home all day. I both welcomed it and dreaded it. I tried not to think about it.

Then, the week before the term ended, there was a telephone call from the school. As soon as the teacher announced herself, my knees began to tremble and there was a rushing sound in my ears. I sank down on a chair, knowing the next blow had fallen.

'They weren't unsupervised—' The teacher was both apologetic and on the defensive. 'She just fell awkwardly. It could have happened to anyone—'

But it had happened to Tessa.

I met them at the doctor's surgery. Tessa was already inside having the plaster cast put on her arm. I went into the office and, reverting to an earlier age, she climbed into my lap as soon as the doctor had finished.

'Not serious at all,' the doctor assured me. 'A nice clean break. Fortunately she's left-handed, so it won't be too difficult for her.'

Tessa hid her face against my shoulder and didn't say a word.

Timothy, white-faced and shaken, looked up as we came out of the office. One of the teachers was with him, not the one who had telephoned, I think.

'I'll drive you home,' she said quickly.

'Thank you,' I said. 'That's very kind.'

All the way home, Tessa didn't speak. Neither did Timothy. They huddled close to me. The teacher talked compulsively and I got all the details—several times. Tessa had simply slipped on the stairs. She had fallen awkwardly. It was unfortunate, but it was not the school's fault. It could have happened to anyone.

'Yes,' I said.

'She was very good,' the teacher said in parting. 'She didn't cry at all.'

In the house, I put the kettle on for tea. When I sat down for a moment, Tessa climbed into my lap again, awkwardly, the cast and sling hampering her.

'Poor baby.' I cuddled her. 'It was a rotten thing to happen, but it will heal. Does it hurt very much?'

'It doesn't matter.' She sighed from a pain too deep for tears and looked up at me. 'Nothing good is ever going to happen to us again, is it, Mummy?'

That night I rang Celia and made the arrangements.

CHAPTER 2

We stepped out of the terminal at Logan Airport into a heat so incredible it was like a slap in the face.

'Like walking into an oven, isn't it?' one of my fellow passengers asked cheerfully.

I agreed. I had never realized before how apt the expression was. Squinting against the blazing sun, we hurried towards the car park.

Celia had been waiting for us just beyond the Customs barrier. I was surprised to see that she was alone, then remembered that, of course, Patrick must be at work. Somehow, I had had the impression that they were both going to meet us.

'Hurry up—' Celia wasted little time on preliminaries. She looked and sounded more Americanized than she had on the telephone. 'If we hurry, we can get out of the city before we get caught up in the rush hour.'

The automobile was another oven; we opened the doors and rolled down the windows to try to let it cool a bit while we loaded our luggage into it. Not until we began to move did the rush of air give an impression of coolness.

'You're looking very well.' We told each other the obligatory social lies. Celia looked awful; she was painfully thin and there was a nervous tic at the corner of her mouth that had never been there before.

'You look marvellous yourself.' Celia lit a fresh cigarette from the stub and crushed the old one out in an overflowing ashtray. She had never been a chain-smoker before, either.

'Thank you.' I looked terrible and I knew it. I'd had no sleep last night and little for the past several nights. The task of putting the house in fit order for strangers to walk into and begin living there had almost been beyond me. In the end, we had piled all personal effects into one room and locked the door. I had left a welcoming letter on the kitchen table explaining this and fully expected to find a similar letter awaiting me in our new quarters. It was the only way of dealing with that problem.

Celia threaded the long car through the traffic expertly and we broke free on to a highway stretched across flat saltmarshes. The children perched on the edge of the back seat, excitedly pointing out sights of interest to each other. There wasn't much to see except an endless series of fast-food drive-ins, but that was enough for them. The novelty of it all would keep them happy and occupied throughout the journey.

I was on the edge of the passenger seat myself, but for a different reason. It was one thing to comprehend intellectually that the traffic drove on the opposite side of the road; it was more difficult to encompass emotion-ally—especially when we soared up the sweeping curve of a hill and I fully expected us to crash into an unseen car mounting the rise from the other direction.

Was that what had happened to John? It had never occurred to me before, but there had been several fatal accidents in England which had eventually been blamed on Americans or Continentals driving on their accustomed side of the road and colliding with native-born citizens going about their lawful business in the correct manner—and killing them.

The police had never been able to trace the killer car, despite finding a generous scraping of paint from the vehicle along the body of John's car. I wondered if they had ever thought of the possibility of a foreigner being responsible; someone who had undoubtedly driven straight to the nearest car ferry and gone back across the Channel as speedily as possible.

Would they think I was neurotic and possibly unbalanced if I wrote to them and suggested the possibility? Did I care what they thought?

'We'll stop for a bite to eat along the way—' Celia swung the car on to another road, heading inland. 'You won't want to be bothered about cooking a meal tonight.'

And neither will I. Not that I blamed her; it was quite true that neither of us would feel like cooking and serving a meal after the rigours of the day. Presumably Patrick and Luke would have made their own arrangements for the evening meal.

We drove into an area of lush farmland dotted with white clapboard houses. Although the architecture was unfamiliar, the terrain was strongly reminiscent of home and I could readily understand why this corner of the New World had been called New England.

'Look at that!' The children were more interested in spotting the differences than identifying the similarities. They watched with awe as a beached clipper ship hove to on the horizon and slid past, only at the last moment revealing itself as a roadside restaurant.

'We'll stop soon,' Celia said comfortingly, mis-interpreting their interest. 'We haven't reached the place with the best ice cream yet. Although,' honesty compelled her to add, 'practically any ice cream here is better than the kind you get.'

'We can get American ice cream now,' I said, 'and it's very good. Very pricey, thought.'

'What isn't, these days?' she sighed.

There was a moment of silence in acknowledgement of this universal truth. I relaxed and closed my eyes. I felt as though I had run a marathon and just crossed the finishing line by using the last of my reserve strength.

The important thing was that I had pulled the children with me to a place of refuge. Even if I were to break down now, they would be safe with Celia. She could look after them and provide the stability I might lack for a while—

Celia screamed, slammed on the brakes and burst into tears.

'My arm! My arm!' Tessa screamed. The children had been thrown against the back of the front seat by the sudden braking.

'Tessa—Celia—' I didn't know which one to comfort first.

'It's all right.' Timothy put his arm round his sister. 'You just bumped it, Tessa. You couldn't break it again, the cast protects it.'

'I was frightened.' Tessa leaned against her brother, whimpering. 'It hurts.'

'Celia!' I turned to my sister. 'What on earth possessed you?'

'The dog!' she sobbed. 'Didn't you see it? I nearly hit it. It ran right in front of me. I nearly hit it!' She went on sobbing wildly.

'But you didn't hit it,' Timothy pointed out reasonably. 'You missed it by a mile. It's all right—' He glanced at me uneasily, obviously remembering a car that had not missed. 'It's all right,' he said again, more tentatively this time.

Perhaps that was what Celia was remembering, too.

She was taking deep breaths, fighting for control, but not winning the battle.

'Look—!' I tried to defuse the situation by providing distraction. 'Look at that fantastic restaurant over there! Why don't we pull in there and have our ice cream now?'

Ahead of us, a building in the shape of a white whale stretched along the highway, a manic mechanical figure perched atop it waving a harpoon. The sign proclaimed: CAPTAIN AHAB'S ARCTIC ICE CREAM.

Tessa gulped a couple of times and shook off Timothy's arm, craning forward for a better view.

'Come on,' I coaxed brightly, as though Celia were one of the children. 'There's plenty of room in the parking lot—' We were blocking the centre lane of the highway and there were cars coming along behind us.. 'Let's just drive over there. I'd love to see what they've done with the inside, wouldn't you?'

'I'd like an ice cream, Mummy,' Tessa said. 'So would Timothy.'

'And so would I.' I spoke firmly and was relieved to see Celia dab at her eyes and slide the car into motion again. She cut across the nearside lane of traffic and pulled smoothly into Captain's Ahab's parking lot.

'You know—' Celia wanted to provide her own distraction now. 'That's something we must do while you're here. Go on a Whale Watch.'

'What's that?' Timothy was intrigued.

'Just what it says—watching whales. The whales have their summer feeding grounds right off the New England coast. About fifteen different varieties of whale swim up to the Stellwagen Bank to feed all through the summer. You can take Whale Watch boats out to the feeding grounds and watch them.'

'Truly?' Timothy glanced at me as though suspecting some adult mockery. 'You can really see them?'

'Sightings guaranteed,' Celia assured him. 'They have a

spotter airplane up over the Stellwagen Bank and it radios
the location of the whales to the ships. We went last year
and Luke was mad about it. He wants to go again, but
we've been waiting for you. We'll arrange it after your jet-
lag has worn off. Now let's go and have our ice-cream.'

The interior of the restaurant was less inventive than
the exterior. It leaned heavily on fishing nets, lobster pots
and the inevitable harpoons. The menu was pleasantly
exotic, however.

Timothy ordered a Moby Dick, which turned out to be
a banana split coated in whipped cream with two dots of
chocolate for eyes. Tessa opted for a Three-Masted
Schooner, three peaks of ice cream surmounted, dis-
appointingly, by white plastic sails. I had an Ahab's
Dream, a mound of vanilla ice cream sinking into a sea of
blueberry sauce with marshmallow fluff whitecaps.

Celia had a cup of black coffee and three more
cigarettes.

The sun was dipping in the sky as we took the final
turning to Edgemarsh Lake. Celia hadn't hurried. There
had been moments when I had received the impression
that she was not anxious to arrive. I had begun to wonder
if there were something wrong with the Harper house; if,
perhaps, it looked better by darkness and Celia wanted to
deposit us there in the gloom and make her escape before
we got a chance to look around.

'It's Smalltown, USA,' Celia said, 'but we like it. I could
never live in a city again.'

She drove down Main Street and it was charming. Too
charming? I found myself peering at the white-painted
buildings suspiciously, as though there might be no
substance behind them, as though we might have strayed
on to a film set. However, lights were beginning to glow
behind ruffle-curtained windows and in the plate-glass
windows of old houses converted into shops, providing

evidence of life within.

'It gets dark earlier on this side of the world,' Celia said. 'I had a hard time getting used to it. Even at Midsummer, it's quite dark by about nine-thirty.' She gave an involuntary shudder. 'That's one of the things I don't like—so many hours of darkness, even at the height of summer. Especially now—'

She broke off and concentrated on several intricate turns that made me feel we were heading into the heart of a maze. I had a despairing moment when I feared we might never find our way out of it again.

The broad well-lighted street was left behind; we were in a dark twisting road that narrowed as we went along. It was still a two-lane thoroughfare—but only just. Houses were fewer and either unoccupied or owned by people who were going to wait until all traces of light had gone before they began using electricity. I was familiar with the legendary New England thrift.

'There are a lot of summer cottages up here,' Celia said reassuringly. 'The owners only come for weekends right now. The season doesn't start properly until after the Fourth of July, then it goes on until after Labor Day. Some people keep coming for weekends through September and into October if the weather holds fair.'

'It's been perfect today. In fact—' With the trip pending, I had begun paying close attention to the foreign weather reports in the daily newspapers. 'I gather you've been having good weather for quite a while.'

'Too good.' Celia frowned into the gloom. 'We'd welcome some rain. Everything is getting too dry. This early in the summer, the worst of the heat hasn't hit us yet. If we don't get a few good soakings before then—' She broke off and took a final turning in a burst of speed, drawing up before a large house set well back from the road.

'Here we are,' she said thankfully. 'Here's your home

for the summer.'

'*All* of it?' Timothy asked in awe. We stared at it in amazement and not a little unease.

'It's bigger than I thought it would be,' I found my voice at last. 'Ours is just a semi-detached.' I was swept by compunction for the innocent Harpers who, at this very moment, might be arriving at the door of our house and wondering if they could squeeze into such small quarters. 'What will they think—?'

'Oh, Nancy and Arnold won't mind,' Celia said airily. 'I've already explained to them that it won't be as big as they're used to and Nancy was quite pleased. Sometimes I think the housework gets on top of her. Arnold won't even notice and the kids will enjoy the novelty.'

The house was dark, which rather surprised me. I had thought that Patrick, since he hadn't been at the airport, might have been waiting at the house to greet us. It seemed, however, that he was going to leave Celia to do all the honours.

'Come along—' She opened her door and stepped out briskly. 'I've got the keys. Let's get the luggage inside and I'll show you round, then . . .' She hesitated. 'Then I'll leave you to settle in and I—I'll come over for coffee in the morning and drive you round the local spots of interest.'

'Oh?' I couldn't hide my surprise and disappointment. I had been looking forward to a long gossip with Celia after we had put the children to bed.

'I'm sorry—' She turned the pale blur of her face away as she led the way up the path. 'I must get back to Patrick . . . he . . . isn't well.'

'I'm sorry.' I apologized in turn. 'I hadn't realized. What—?'

'Later . . .' Her footsteps echoed on the wooden steps and across the wooden porch. 'Tomorrow . . .' She opened a screen door, then I heard the scrape of a key in the lock and the inner door swung open. Celia stepped inside, there was the snap of a switch and light flooded the porch.

'Look—' Timothy lingered at the top of the steps, surveying the porch. 'They've got rocking-chairs out here—and a hammock swing. And—'

'Hurry up,' Celia said. 'We don't want mosquitoes getting into the house. They've got those, too.'

'I like the hanging baskets.' Unburdened by luggage, Tessa skipped into the hallway. I went back to the car for the rest of our cases.

Celia had gone through the house snapping on lights. When I entered, the screen door slamming behind me, I found everyone in the large cosy living-room that ran parallel with the long wide porch outside. Two wide windows faced on to the porch and I could quite see how convenient it would be on rainy days to send the children out to play on the porch and still be able to keep an eye on them from the living-room. If we ever had any rainy days here. I said as much to Celia.

'That's a proper veranda,' she corrected me. 'The old-timers still call it a pee-azza.' She gave every letter full value, accentuating a Yankee twang. 'Most of the older houses have them. I can see that they're quite attractive— if you like that sort of thing. We have a modern Cape Cod Cottage with a patio, ourselves.'

'I know. You've sent me pictures. I'm looking forward to seeing it.'

'You'd better see this house first.' I winced inwardly as Celia stubbed out a cigarette in a delicate glass bowl. She did not succeed in extinguishing it completely. She sailed out of the room without a backward glance at the thin acrid wisps of smoke still curling upwards from the smouldering stub. I hesitated, but the sides of the bowl were curved and steep; the cigarette could be left to burn itself out safely. Besides, she had halted in the doorway and was now looking back at me impatiently, waiting for me to follow her. It could look too pointed—perhaps reproachful—if I stopped to extinguish the cigarette while she was watching.

'Bring your cases,' Celia directed. 'We'll start upstairs. You can leave your things in the bedrooms.'

I picked up Tessa's small case and my own; I would carry the heavy cases up later when the children couldn't watch. Already, Timothy was fretting because he was not big enough to manage them and Tessa was upset because her arm prevented her from carrying even a light case.

'Rosemary, you'll have the master bedroom, of course.' Celia flung open the door and switched on the light.

'It's beautiful.' I looked around the opulent room thus revealed. A dark red richly-patterned Oriental rug covered the gleaming pine floorboards, an enormous double bed dominated the room, reflected in both the dressing-table mirror and a full-length pier glass in one corner. The ubiquitous rocking-chair was also present.

'I knew you'd like it,' Celia said with satisfaction. 'Now, let's get the children settled. Tessa, you'll have Donna's room. Timothy, you'll have Donald's.'

After that, it was a whirlwind tour. Celia raced us from room to room without giving us time to take them in.

'The bathroom . . . the guest rooms—' Celia opened doors briefly and closed them again—'but you won't need to worry about that. You don't know anyone, so you won't be having guests.' She shut the last door with finality and was half way down the stairs before we could follow.

On the ground floor, she rushed us from living-room to Arnold's study, to dining-room, to kitchen—and then down into the cellar.

Somewhere along the way, she had found time to light another cigarette but not to find an ashtray. A trail of ashes marked our progress through the house, not deliberately flicked off, just dropping off from their own weight and unnoticed by Celia in her overriding preoccupation.

'When I first came to this country,' Celia told us, 'they called basement rooms like this the Rumpus Room. Now it seems to be the Playroom.'

'Ping-pong!' Timothy shouted joyously, advancing on the table in the middle of the room. A darts board was hanging on the farther wall, a folding bridge table in a corner held a partially-completed jigsaw puzzle, outdoor sports equipment huddled in another corner. Tessa raised the lid of an old chest perforated with holes and discovered a cache of games.

'Do they have giant woodworm here, Mummy?' she asked fearfully, studying the holes.

'We don't have woodworm at all,' Celia snapped indignantly. 'Arnold drilled those holes especially, so that there wouldn't be any danger if the kids played hide-and-seek and one of them got into the chest. There have been tragedies in the past . . .' Her voice trailed off.

'From time immemorial,' I agreed. 'Didn't Tennyson do a poem about it—or was it Sir Walter Scott?'

'Probably both,' Celia said. 'It was a popular theme. No, Timothy—' she called. 'You can't go in there.'

'Out of bounds.' Timothy read out a hand-lettered notice pinned to a side door.

'Nancy apologizes for that—' Celia relayed the message. 'She's piled all their clothing and private items in there and locked the door. She said it seemed the easiest thing to do.'

'Oh, good. I'm glad she's done that because it's exactly what we did. She won't mind finding a locked room in our house, then.'

'You'll find the key on the key ring—in case of emergency, but you shouldn't have to use it.'

'That's right. I left the key—just in case. The washing-machine overflows occasionally and water has been known to seep under the door. I'd appreciate it if she mopped up in there before any damage was done.'

'The cubicle over there—' Celia was uninterested in my domestic problems—'is a shower stall, so that you can rinse the sand off before you go upstairs if you've been swimming in the lake.

'Never mind those steps—' She gestured and another mound of ash fell to the floor. I wasn't going to worry about it this time—the basement floor was cement. 'They lead up to an old-fashioned bulkhead door—you have to go half way up the steps and throw it open. It used to be the only outside entrance to the cellar, but Nancy and Arnold had a proper door put in over there—' Another gesture, another heap of ash. 'No one ever uses the bulkhead any more, but they never got round to having it sealed off. You'll get a better idea of the layout when you see it in the daylight.'

'I'm willing to wait.' I could hardly articulate the words for the yawn. The children seemed to be more alert. Timothy had found a ping-pong ball and paddle and was looking around hopefully for an opponent. Tessa had drifted over to the jigsaw puzzle and was becoming absorbed in it, something she could do easily with one hand.

'You could all do with an early night.' Celia led the way back upstairs and headed firmly for the front door. 'I'll be over in the morning. Get a good night's sleep.'

At the open door she turned back suddenly and hugged me. 'Oh, Rosemary, I'm so glad you're here!'

CHAPTER 3

Hi, Rosemary, Tessa and Timothy—Welcome to Cranberry Lane. I hope you'll like it here. I just know we're going to love your place . . .

I had seen the note waiting for us on the kitchen table, but Celia had been dismissive. 'You can read it later.'
Later had arrived. The children were bathed and in their pyjamas, having a glass of milk and some sweet biscuits—we must learn to say 'cookies', as was printed on the packet—before going to bed. I was reading the letter aloud.

I won't try to put everything in this letter or you'll be up all night reading it. I've left notes around the house re things you ought to know about. You'll find them as you need them—I hope!

We nodded at each other. I had done much the same. The washing-machine had had a special note of warning.

I've explained to Errol that you're going to be his temporary family for the summer and he said 'Okay'. He's an absolute love and very easy-going and I know you'll love him as much as we do. Just one thing—please don't let him have canned cat food more than twice a week. It doesn't agree with him after that. He usually eats what we eat—he gets a lot of mileage out of scraps. One other thing—you'll find his brush and a can of flea powder in the back entry. Sorry about that—but with the woods right behind us and the hot weather, there's no way he can avoid fleas.
I usually water the flowers in the hanging baskets every second day and just talk to them a little while

you're doing it—it makes them grow. The garden
should be watered once a week and in-between if it
needs it. Unless there's a drought and the water
restrictions are in force. You'll read about it in the
local paper, of which, please save all copies for me
so that I'll be able to catch up with the news when I get
back. Don't worry about buying it—we subscribe and it
will be delivered every Friday. It's all paid for, so
don't let the paper boy try to tell you any different—
I don't quite trust him . . .

Fortunately the children were distracted by a noise
outside and didn't notice my voice trailing off as the letter
became both confidential and libellous. I decided I would
finished reading it when they were in bed.

'What's that?' Tessa asked as the noise came again, a
high, piercing, demanding summons at the back door.

'It must be the cat—' Timothy set down his glass of
milk and dashed for the door. He opened it and fell back
in awe at the creature who marched past him.

'Is that a cat?' Tessa eyed it doubtfully. It was a good
question.

The brute was twice the size of our lovely Esmond; a
burly, thick-necked, square-headed animal, given an
unexpectedly rakish look by the fact that the tip of one
ear had evidently been chewed off in some private dispute
of long ago. A patch of tiger fur was growing back at the
base of his long waving tail, but had not reached the
length of the rest of his fur yet. He had great flashing
eyes—one blue and one amber. He paused inside the
doorway and regarded us thoughtfully.

'Errol?' I asked tentatively. 'Are you Errol?'

The monster leered affably and advanced into the
room. Half way across, he lowered himself into a crouch,
brought up a hind leg and attacked the mangled ear with
such vigour that he seemed in danger of scratching off

what remained of it.

'Shall I bring in the flea powder?' Timothy asked helpfully.

'Not now. Errol will just have to put up with it until morning. We'll tackle it then. He must be used to fleas.'

Errol finished scratching and resumed his interrupted progress. He halted in front of the refrigerator and stared at it pointedly.

'I think he's hungry,' Tessa said.

'I wouldn't be surprised,' I said faintly. Errol looked capable of eating a cow-and-a-half at each meal, skin, bones and all. It was difficult to think of him as having a delicate digestive system. 'I'm afraid he'll have to settle for a tin of cat food tonight, though. We'll go shopping tomorrow and get in some supplies—'

The telephone rang and we all jumped. 'It must be Celia.' I went to answer it.

'I'll feed Errol,' Timothy said. 'I've found the tin-opener.'

'Hello?' Absently, I registered the note left for me on the telephone pad. It was like an unexpected nudge in the ribs.

Useful telephone numbers: Fire Department 341; Doctor 748; Electrician 225; Plumber 576; May's Mini Market 963 (more expensive than the supermarket, but they'll deliver COD if you phone in an order) . . .

Then a list of names which meant nothing to me now but presumably would at some future date.

'Hello?' I realized that I had been waiting for a reply. 'Hello . . . Celia?'

There was a click at the other end, then the dial tone. Odd . . . and there was something odd about the note on the telephone pad, too.

'Who was it, Mummy?' Tessa asked as I went back into the kitchen.

'A wrong number,' I said. They might have apologized. Or perhaps it was someone who had been startled to get an English voice answering. Surely, though, all the Harpers' friends must know about the house swap. If any of them had rung in an absent moment, why hadn't they identified themselves and explained? It would have taken only a moment and would have been the courteous thing to do.

The children lost interest. Bemused, they were watching Errol as he gulped down the cat food. He was a noisy eater. As though he felt my disapproval, he raised his head and glared at me. He had a fine line in disapproval himself. He turned his head and concentrated on Tessa's glass of milk.

'I think he wants a drink,' Timothy said. 'Shall I give him some milk?'

'Why don't you?' I decided against voicing an opinion that Errol looked as though he might prefer straight whisky.

The telephone rang again. This time it *was* Celia.

'Did you ring a few minutes ago?' I asked.

'No, I just got in. I wanted to remind you that the cat was around somewhere and would expect to be let in and fed.'

'Thank you, we've already found him. At least, I think it's a cat.'

'Errol is a Maine coon cat—they're the large economy size.'

'Except when you're feeding them.' Errol was making short work of a tin which would have done Esmond for two meals.

'Fortunately, he likes vegetables. When you're cooking, just toss an extra potato and another handful of peas or whatever into the pot for him. Nancy started him as she meant him to go on when he was just a kitten—'

'Celia, is everything all right?' She was burbling on far too much about the blasted cat. It wasn't like her. Or had it been so long since we'd met that I no longer knew what she was like?

'Of course. Why shouldn't it be?'

'You said something about Patrick not being well . . ."

I frowned absently at the message pad; I could tell from the quality of the silence at the other end of the line that she hadn't liked my answer.

'Nothing dramatic is going to happen suddenly. It isn't that kind of unwell.' Her voice was too crisp. She was trying to convince herself as well as me.

'You asked if I'd rung earlier—' She changed the subject abruptly. 'Did you have a . . . an unidentified caller? What did they say?'

'They didn't say a word. Just listened for a moment and then rang off. Why? Has Nancy been having trouble with telephone calls?' Inheriting an obscene caller was all I needed. Welcome to America!

'No, no, of course not!' Had she denied it too quickly? 'It must have been one of her friends who'd forgotten she'd already left.'

'I thought of that. Rather rude friends, hasn't she? They might have spoken and apologized. The other thing I thought of,' I added wickedly, 'was that perhaps it was burglars ringing to find out if the house was empty.'

'You *will* lock the doors tonight?' Celia didn't laugh. 'Front and back—and check that all the windows are latched. One can't be too careful these days.'

'Oh, Celia—' I caught back a yawn—'of course, I'll lock up properly. I'm not a child.'

'You're dead on your feet.' Her voice softened. 'Get to bed, the lot of you.' She rang off.

I yawned again, not even trying to restrain it. She was right. It was bed for all of us. I'd lock up all right, but if burglars got in tonight, they'd just have to take anything they wanted.

They could start with Errol. Having finishing his meal, he was sharpening his claws on the leg of the lovely maplewood kitchen table.

'Stop that at once!' I darted at him, hand upraised threateningly. 'I'm sure you're not allowed to do that when your family are home.'

Muttering darkly, he stalked over to the door and demanded his freedom. I let him out, slammed the door behind him and locked it; while I was at it, I checked that the kitchen windows were latched.

Then I gazed with dismay at the fresh raw scars on the table leg, We hadn't been in the house one night yet and already there was visible damage. It wasn't our fault, but it was there.

'Oh dear,' I moaned, kneeling and rubbing vainly at the scars. 'And we were going to be so careful!' Even through my guilt, I wondered what was happening back at *our* house. Were the Harper twins as bad as their yobbo cat? What damage would we find waiting for us when we returned?

'It doesn't show much.' Timothy spat on his fingers and rubbed the scars. 'Not when you're standing up.'

'Don't worry, Mummy,' Tessa comforted. 'We can get something to put on it and polish it every day and the scratches will go away.'

'I can't worry about anything more tonight,' I admitted. 'Let's go up to bed.'

Once the children were tucked up in bed, I found that I couldn't settle down myself. I paced the floor of the luxurious master bedroom; the double bed waited. I had not approached it; I could not. At this hour, in the darkness, it seemed to represent everything I had lost.

I crossed to the window and stood looking out over the humming air-conditioning unit which occupied the lower part of the window. Immediately below me was the roof of the veranda. Beyond it, I could see the path leading up from the road. The trees stirred silently, there must be a breeze. I tugged at the window but it refused to budge; the air-conditioning unit ruled, no natural air could be allowed in to disrupt its smooth operation.

Restlessly I left the room and checked on the children—they were both sleeping soundly. From Tessa's room, I could hear the predatory yowl of a marauding cat somewhere out in the woods. Errol, no doubt. I was beginning to see why he had been so named.

Tonight I was not amused. Like a prowling cat myself, I left Tessa's room and went down the corridor, exploring the rooms I had glimpsed so briefly on Celia's whirlwind tour.

The sewing-room; an electric sewing-machine, the dark sinister shadow of a dressmaker's dummy, a Victorian sewing basket on a pedestal. Evidently Nancy was the domestic type. I closed the door softly; I'd have no reason to open it again for the remainder of our visit.

At the end of the hallway, I opened the door on enchantment. A guest room so welcoming it seemed to reach out invisible arms and draw me inside. It was decorated in New England Colonial style, delicate floral-sprigged wallpaper, braided rugs on the polished pinewood floor, a light maple rocking-chair beside a bookcase full of well-read books, a large window set into the eaves so that there was a wide, comfortable window-seat one could curl up on. And the three-quarter-size brass bed was also wide and comfortable, inviting without being daunting. I could feel at home in here.

I retrieved my suitcases from the master bedroom, turning off the air-conditioning as I left, and moved in at once. This would be my room for the summer.

After unpacking, I knelt on the window-seat and found, as I had hoped when I had noted that it was without an air-conditioning unit, that the window slipped upwards easily. There was a screen on the outside and a cool breeze from the lake immediately wafted into the room.

There was an old-fashioned electric fan on the dressing-table; I flicked the switch and it hummed into action, picking up speed and revolving slowly. On the oppposite side of the dressing-table was a vase of fresh flowers. The oddity surprised me for a moment; there had been no flowers in the master bedroom.

With a mental shrug, I tossed back the patchwork quilt covering the bed. A white envelope lay on the pillow. I was beginning to be familiar with those envelopes by now.

Dear Rosemary,

I thought you might prefer this room. I know I would, if I were in your shoes. It's where I put my favorite guests.

Look in the bedside tabouret for a little nightcap. It's homemade—Pixie Toller's specialty. (You'll meet her soon, if you haven't already.)

Have a nice summer—

Nancy

The tabouret held a small decanter labelled elderberry brandy and a plastic box containing thin crispy vanilla biscuits.

Shamelessly ignoring the fact that I had already cleaned my teeth and had no intention of cleaning them again, I partook of both. Both were delicious.

I slid into bed and turned out the light. In the darkness I was conscious of the small night sounds outside, no longer drowned by the noise of the air-conditioner. The wind rustled the trees, grasshoppers sang, frogs croaked softly; a soothing and pleasing lullaby.

Just as I drifted off to sleep, I identified the disquieting element I had subconsciously noticed in the telephone list. The order of importance was wrong.

I was a woman on her own with two children, one of whom had a broken arm.

Why, then, did the Fire Department lead the list of emergency numbers instead of the Doctor?

CHAPTER 4

It wasn't the dreams that were the nightmare, it was the awakening. In sleep, John was there again. We were laughing together, planning a holiday, talking about a future beyond that. We turned to each other with love and joy . . .

I don't know what woke me. I opened my eyes to bright sunlight and the unfamiliar room and slowly the joy drained out of me and the bleak grey sadness took its place. John was dead and I was left to face another day.

There was no point in lying there. I threw back the sheet and automatically walked over to the window. I could see now that my room was right at the back of the house, over the kitchen. Beneath the window was the slanted wooden bulkhead door which opened into the cellar. Beyond that was the spacious back yard, then the thick ring of woodland, mostly pines and maples, and beyond that the glittering blue of Edgemarsh Lake. The sky was clear and cloudless, the birds sang. It was a beautiful day in a beautiful country.

And what should I do in Illyria?

'No! No! Stop it!' The childrens' voices shrieked out in anguish from the kitchen below me. I ran downstairs, not waiting to put on my dressing-gown, terrified of what I might find.

I burst into the kitchen and was relieved to find Tessa and Timothy safe, although furious and upset. There was a delicious fragrance in the air, which seemed to be part of the problem.

'Mummy! Mummy!' Tessa threw herself into my arms, sobbing. 'We were cooking breakfast. We wanted to surprise you. We were going to bring you breakfast in bed.'

'We made scrambled eggs—' Timothy glowered. 'Only that rotten old Errol got up on the table and ate them all!'

'Oh, darlings—' I tried not to laugh, as much a hysterical reaction as Tessa's tears. 'Never mind. We'll cook some more and we'll be more careful this time. Remember Nancy told us that Errol eats everything we eat—she should have warned us "especially if he gets there first".'

'Rotten old Errol!' Tessa echoed Timothy, a faint smile breaking through.

'Rotten to the core,' I agreed. A trail of greasy egg fragments stretched across the table from the empty plate, across the floor and under the stove. As we gazed at the mute evidence, there came a tremendous belch from beneath the stove.

'Perhaps it will disagree with him,' I said hopefully, then rescinded my hopes. 'Errol—' I called sharply. 'Come out. You can't be sick under there—' I dashed over to open the back door. 'Come on—outside! Quick!'

There was no response from Errol. I left the back door open—the screen door was still closed but could be opened quickly enough—and walked over to the stove.

'Errol?' Silence. I crouched and looked under the stove. He was curled up into a tight ball and out like a light, plainly exhausted by the night's excesses.

'Is he all right?' Timothy asked doubtfully.

'Your cooking didn't kill him, if that's what you mean." I straightened up. 'I should think he'll sleep for most of the day now. We can forget him for a while. Now . . . what's in the pantry for breakfast?'

Fortunately, the children did not remember their Uncle Patrick. I was hard-pressed to hide my shock at the sight of him as I opened the door; they never could have managed it.

His cheekbones jutted out from the dark hollows under his eyes; his short-sleeved shirt and trousers had been bought for a larger man; his eyes had a haunted look and his painful smile did not quite reach them.

We may both be widows soon. Perhaps the thought could be read too easily in my own eyes. Celia caught my arm and drew me to one side.

'It's nerves, that's all,' she said urgently. 'Just nerves. The business, is going through a bad patch right now. A lot of businesses are. If we can just last through the summer . . .'

Patrick had gone into the living-room while we hung back in the hallway. Now he appeared in the doorway and looked at Celia questioningly.

'Yes, dear, we're coming,' Celia said, too brightly. We followed him into the living-room.

'It's good to see you again, Rosemary,' he said. He looked around the room with vague dissatisfaction, as though there were someone else he would rather see. I remembered that I was in his cousin Nancy's house and wondered if he were missing her already. 'The kids, too. They sure have grown, haven't they? What are they now, six and eight?'

'Time goes on,' I said. 'Timothy's nine and Tessa is seven. Y—' I broke off just in time. *You've changed, too.* If he realized it, he wouldn't appreciate being reminded of it.

'We thought we'd drive you around the Lake this morning,' Celia said quickly. 'We'll stop at Camp Mohigonquin and collect Luke and his friend Dexter—they're joining us for lunch. That will give you a chance to see what it's like and have a word with Greg

Carter, he's the Camp Administrator and Senior Counsellor, about enrolling Tessa and Timothy as day campers.'

'I'll have to think that one over,' I said firmly. 'It's much too soon to make any sort of decision. We've only just arrived.' With distance and the passing of time, I had almost forgotten Celia's tendency to arrange every moment of everyone's life for them. Her success in getting me over here had evidently gone to her head. I would need to keep reasserting my intention—and right—to order my own life and the lives of my children, even though she was more familiar with this strange new country than I was.

'Oh, all right.' She acknowledged grudgingly that a warning shot had just been fired across her bows. 'But you can't delay too long. The summer people will start flooding in next week and there won't be any places left. *They* know a good thing when they see it.'

'I haven't seen it yet,' I reminded her.

'Let's get going, then.' Patrick leaped to his feet, jingling his car keys. 'We've brought the station wagon so that we can fit everyone in. Unless you'd like to try out the Harpers' car? You could follow us over—'

'No!' I froze at the thought. I hadn't driven since John's accident. I had no wish ever to get behind the wheel of a car again. 'No, I'm not used to the idea of driving on the wrong side of the road. Give me some time to get acclimatized.'

'You ought to get used to a right-hand drive as soon as possible,' Celia put in swiftly, sensing weakness. 'It's a full-time job hereabouts ferrying children to their various destinations.'

'All the more reason for me not to get caught up in it. This is supposed to be a holiday.'

'She's got you there,' Patrick said. 'Come on, everybody. All aboard for Camp Mohigonquin.'

Camp Mohigonquin stood on a hillside on the opposite side of the lake. It would have been about a mile if one were to row across; going by road, curving through woods and past summer cottages, the distance was about six miles. We turned in at the gates and bumped up a rough track.

At the end of it were half a dozen long low wooden cabins, as many large canvas tents, all clustered around a central clearing with a flagpole from which fluttered the American flag. The camp enclosure was bordered by a tennis court, an archery range and a sports track. The remaining side was clear sweep down to the lakeshore beach; there was also a boathouse and a small dock with several canoes moored to it.

A mixed doubles match occupied the tennis courts and an informal race was in progress on the sports track. Timothy's eyes had begun to sparkle as he looked around.

While we watched, a group of children erupted from one of the tents and war-whooped their way down the slope to pile into the waiting canoes. Tessa gave a little sniff and cradled her arm protectively.

Timothy might be in his element here, but it didn't hold much promise for my poor little broken-winged bird.

'There's Luke!' Celia spotted her son and led us over to the archery range. 'Luke, we're here!'

I caught my breath as the tall gangling blond boy turned and smiled at me with my father's eyes and my mother's mouth.

'Yes, I thought you'd catch that,' Celia said softly. 'He does, doesn't he?'

I nodded, knowing that we mustn't mention it in front of him. Nothing annoys children more than having pieces of what they consider their personal anatomy parcelled out and attributed to ancestors they have never known. Tessa always grew twitchy if anyone pointed out that her hair grew in a widow's peak just like her paternal grandmother's. After registering the observation the first half-dozen times, she had insisted on wearing a fringe. When she was older, she would appreciate the advantage; right now, it seemed a denial of her own personality when anyone mentioned the source of her dramatic hairline.

The cousins appraised each other silently while Celia made the introductions. A tall, lean, bronzed man stood by.

'And this is Gregory Carter—' Celia finished, indicating him. 'The Camp Administrator.'

'Just Greg, please.' He flashed white perfect teeth and captured my hand in a strong firm handshake. 'I've been hearing about you people. Glad to have you aboard.'

He shook hands with Timothy, but Tessa shrank back, afraid to trust her remaining good hand to this athletic giant. He hesitated, then reached out and tousled her hair. She didn't like that, either. She sent me a worried look.

'We're not quite aboard,' I said a trifle tartly. 'Celia may have given you the wrong impression. We haven't decided what we're doing yet.'

'Oh, for heaven's sake,' Celia said under her breath. 'Do you have to make an issue of it?'

'Oh-oh, guess I put my foot in my mouth again.' Greg smiled even more broadly, demonstrating that there was plenty of room for his foot in there despite all those large gleaming teeth. 'Look, we weren't trying to railroad you into anything. Why, you haven't even seen the place yet. Let me show you around.'

He wheeled and strode off, not looking to see if we were following. Celia gave me a little push and started me forward. Luke and Timothy were already on Greg's heels. Patrick seated himself on a tree-stump beside the archery range and appeared to go into a trance.

'Girls' dormitory here—' Greg indicated one of the long

log cabins. 'Boys' dorm over there. Cookhouse—one cooked meal a day, one salad meal, trained dietician supervising. Day campers usually leave at six, but if you'd like them to stay on for the evening meal so that you don't have to bother cooking, that can be arranged.'

'I don't find cooking any bother,' I said coldly. 'I quite enjoy it.'

'Good, good. I wish all the Moms felt that way.' He glanced at my face and moved on quickly. 'Dispensary, with a registered nurse in attendance. She also doubles as a Camp Counsellor, we don't have much for her to do, otherwise. Barring the occasional cuts or scrapes—' This time he glanced at Tessa. 'Accidents will happen.'

'Show her the tents, Greg,' Celia prompted. 'That's where they do crafts and handiwork,' she told me. 'There's bound to be something for Tessa there.'

'Sure, there will,' Greg said heartily. 'This tent is Woodwork: carving, carpentry, that sort of thing. And this tent is Artwork: clays sculpture, pottery, fingerpainting—' His voice took on a coaxing tone as he displayed a bright hotchpotch of colour. 'You could do that okay, Tessa. Most of the kids only use one hand for fingerpainting, anyway.'

Tessa retreated behind me in the face of this direct onslaught, but I saw that a gleam of interest had been kindled in her eyes.

'Then there's weaving, jewellery-making—' He waved a hand, indicating the other tents. 'And over there—' He stopped short, his eyes narrowed.

'Okay, Dexter, front-and-centre!' he snapped. 'What were you doing in there?'

And enormous boy in shorts and T-shirt sidled to a halt in front of us, Billy Bunter to the life. I had the impression that he had come from the cookhouse. His jaws were working rapidly, then his Adam's apple bobbed several times and he spoke:

'Hi, Greg. Hi, Luke, Mrs Meadows. I was just coming to meet you.' He flourished a gold wristwatch under his nose. 'Time for us to be getting along, isn't it?'

'Not so fast, fella—' There was still a steely note in Greg's voice. 'I asked you a question.'

'We ought to get going,' Luke put in hastily, addressing his mother. 'Dad's getting kinda restless.'

'Oh!' Celia whirled to look at Patrick. He was pacing round the tree-stump, jingling his car keys. 'Oh yes! I'm sorry, Greg, but—' She shrugged helplessly.

'Sure, I understand.' The teeth were much in evidence again, but he slanted a look at Dexter that boded ill for him in the future.

'Look, you folks—' He turned back to us, switching on the charm with an almost audible click. 'Look, we're having a cookout tomorrow night. Why don't you come up and be our guests? About eight o'clock. It happens once a week—you'll like it.' He met Tessa's eyes and the coaxing note was back in his voice. 'You can hold a hot dog on a stick over the campfire with one hand, can't you? No problem. We toast marshmallows, too, for dessert. And we have a sing-song. It's fun. You will come, won't you?'

'Well . . .' Both children were looking at me hopefully. I was outnumbered, not that it mattered. I didn't care what I did. It would be as good a way of spending an evening as any other. 'Thank you, we'll look forward to that.'

'Great!' Greg was obviously aching to say something else to Dexter but realized that any further comment might dent the image he wished to project. He turned to Celia. 'I hope you and Patrick will come along, too. Luke is staying on for it and we'd love to have you.'

'Yes . . . thank you,' Celia said vaguely. 'I'll have to see whether Patrick has anything else planned.' She looked anxiously towards her husband and became more decisive. 'We must be going now. We have a one o'clock reservation at Gino's Place.'

'Right!' Greg's teeth flashed again. 'These folks can see the rest of the camp tomorrow. And Dexter—' The teeth just missed grinding together as the mask slipped. 'Cottage cheese salad for you—right, fella?'

'Sure, Greg,' Dexter said unconvincingly. 'What else?'

Gino's Place had been someone else's place first; an Old Homestead converted into a restaurant, keeping as many homelike touches as possible. Gino himself greeted us at the door and led us to a table on the glassed-in side porch.

'My cousin will take care of your table,' he told Patrick. 'Let me know if everything is all right. I think he is nearly trained now. If he continues to be satisfactory, I will promote him to waiting on the inside tables next week. He sulks because he isn't there already, but he's not as good as he thinks he is—not yet.'

'You knew you were going to have a few problems when you imported him from the Old Country,' Patrick said. 'Even though he's shaping up slowly, at least he's shaping up—and you needed him. This is a big place to run.'

'Hah!' Gino laughed shortly, without mirth. 'It is not big enough for Rudolfo—that's the problem. He thought he was coming to be *maître d'* of a great fashionable restaurant. An outpost of The Four Seasons, perhaps. He expected celebrities every night, four star cuisine, hundred dollar bills to light cigars with—'

'The streets paved with gold, eh?' Patrick sighed. 'Do they still believe that?'

'He expected New York,' Gino said flatly. 'He got New Hampshire. He must learn to live with it. Still, this is only his first summer here. Probably he will settle down.'

'Early days yet,' Celia agreed. She glanced at her watch.

'Rudi—' Gino called to a waiter who had just entered.

'The menus for this table, please.' He bowed and left us.

Celia evidently did not feel it incumbent on her to maintain camp discipline. She allowed Dexter to order pork chops and French fries, a lavish salad, sans cottage cheese, came as a side dish but he ignored it.

The air-conditioning was frigid, presumably to encourage an appetite for hot meals. The prices seemed quite reasonable to me, but Patrick surveyed them with a twisted grin.

'I'm not that old,' he said ruefully, 'but I can remember when a dollar bought the Blue Plate Special. These days it doesn't even pay the tip.'

For dessert, the rest of us ordered ice cream, but Dexter continued on his collision course with the maximum of calories.

'I'll have the Crêpes Suzette,' he said casually.

'Will they let you?' Patrick was dubious. 'You're underage and it contains alcohol.'

'The booze will burn off—' Dexter licked his lips— 'when they flambé it. Sure, they'll let me have it. Rudi's made them for me before—he likes making them.'

'Well . . .' Patrick said.

Rudi had no qualms at all. In fact, he was delighted. He wheeled the serving trolley to our table with a flourish, conscious that everyone was watching. Gino hovered in the doorway, checking on the proceedings.

Tessa and Timothy had never seen the dish prepared before and were enthralled. As the flickering blue flames danced over the crêpes, they laughed with glee. Smiling at their reaction, I sought Celia's eyes to share the amusement—and felt a chill that owed nothing to the over-emphatic air-conditioning.

Celia was watching Patrick with a look of unmistakable concern. Patrick was watching the flames with a curious intensity, as though they held him hypnotized.

I looked away quickly, uneasily, and focused on

Dexter. He, too, was staring deep into the miniature blue inferno with more than healthy interest.

Suddenly I wished that we were back in England.

CHAPTER 5

By the time we got back to Cranberry Lane and Patrick and the boys had carried in the groceries, we were exhausted. I felt as though I had spent the day fighting alternating spells of chills and fever—which I had.

After lunch, we had gone shopping. The constant transition from the overpowering heat outdoors to the icy blasts of air-conditioned stores would have been enervating even when uncomplicated by jet-lag. Outside, one longed for the cool interiors of the shops; once inside, it instantly became too much of a good thing. By the time we strolled down the frozen food aisles of the supermarket, with the double chill coming from the freezers on both sides, I began to see why so many shoppers carried light cardigans, despite the heat. I would have been glad of a cardigan myself—and a pair of gloves.

'You've turned off the air-conditioning,' Celia said accusingly as we entered the house. 'That's an English habit you're going to have to lose, or you'll collapse with heat prostration. If you don't care about yourself, think of the children!' She switched on the window unit in the living-room.

'I've put it on low,' she said grudgingly. 'No, stay there—' she waved me back as I started for the stairs. 'I'll turn it on in the bedroom. I can't trust you, other-wise—not until you get acclimatized.'

She darted up the stairs and, after a moment, I heard her footsteps in the master bedroom overhead. I decided not to tell her that I had switched rooms—it would cut out one more argument and make life easier. I'd turn off the air-conditioning up there after she left.

'Where do you want things to go?' Patrick returned from the kitchen looking helpful but inadequate to the situation. 'I've left the bags on the kitchen table.'

'I'll see to them.' I reached the kitchen just as Errol climaxed a mangificent leap by landing lightly on the tabletop with his nose unerringly in the bag containing the fresh fish.

'Down, Errol!' I removed his head from the bag and pushed him towards the edge of the table. He fought me all the way, protesting wildly that I couldn't expect him to leave when the party had just begun.

'Down!' Errol was strong and determined; so was I. We had a brief undignified struggle and then Errol hit the floor. Once down there, he changed tactics and twined sinuously around my ankles, purring of devotion and undying affection.

Nothing is undying, Errol. Nothing . . . and no one . . .

But he had succeeded in making me feel guilty. We had been gone all day and poor Errol had had nothing to eat since the purloined scrambled eggs this morning. Further, I realized that he had been very good. Despite our difference of opinion and the fact that we were practically strangers, he had not even threatened to use his claws. Perhaps Errol *was* a love, as his absent owners claimed.

'All right, I'll get you something,' I said. 'Just let me put this stuff in the freezer.'

We tripped across the floor. I wouldn't have tripped if it weren't for Errol. Recognition of our destination brought him out in fresh paroxysms of affection. I stumbled against the refrigerator and fended him off with one foot while I opened the door.

'*Hi, Rosemary*—' The note was lurking in the freezer

compartment at the top. I looked at it unenthusiastically. This constant unearthing of messages was beginning to make me feel as though I were living with an elbow perpetually sinking into my ribs.

If you need more space, I've cleared a corner of the deep freeze in the garage for you. If you'd like to use any of the food I've left in it, please do. I keep the old blanket beside it in case of electrical failure. Sometimes a thunderstorm knocks down a power line. In which case, I toss the blanket over the deep freeze for a bit of extra insulation until the lines are fixed. It usually doesn't take long, but if it does—'

I pushed the note to the back of the freezer compartment and piled the frozen food on top of it. If the power failed, I'd dig it out later and read the rest of the instructions.

I splashed some milk into Errol's saucer to hold him until I'd finished stowing away the rest of the shopping.

Patrick came back into the kitchen carrying the last two shopping-bags. We seemed to have bought an inordinate amount, but Celia had assured me that it was better to buy in bulk and get enough to last for as long as possible. Apart from which, everything took up so much space—basic supplies seemed to come in 'Large', 'Larger', and 'Large Economy Size' exclusively. Only 'Sample' size looked reasonable to my eyes, but there were few items so modestly packaged.

'That's better.' Celia followed Patrick with the air of a job well done. 'You must remember to keep windows and doors closed or you'll just be trying to cool all outdoors—and it can't be done. Although,' she added grudgingly, 'if it gets cooler in the evenings, you can open the inside front and back doors and let a breeze through. But keep the screen doors closed or the house will be filled with mosquitoes and insects.'

'All right,' I said mendaciously. I intended to turn off all the air-conditioning as soon as she left, although I did take her point about screens and insects. There seemed to be an awful lot of the latter, doubtless they bred excessively in this climate.

'It looks like we're in for a real scorcher this weekend.' Patrick took a glass and sauntered over to the refrigerator. I watched with fascination as he thrust the empty glass into the niche in the outside of the refrigerator door. We had examined it curiously last night but I had refused to allow the children to experiment with the two bracket levers until we knew how they should be used and what would happen. Our funds did not run to replacing broken major appliances.

Patrick pushed the glass briefly against one lever at the back of the niche and a cascade of miniature ice cubes swooshed into the glass. He then filled the glass with iced water from the nozzle poised above the second lever. The action was so automatic that he did not even notice that I was following his movements avidly. *All mod. cons.* I thought guiltily of the refrigerator we had thought so up-to-date and hoped the Harpers hadn't lost the knack of wrestling with old-fashioned ice trays.

'I wish it would rain,' Celia said.

'Spoil the weekend.' Patrick sipped his iced water.

'Not for *us.*" Something in Celia's tone implied the weekend was already spoiled. I wondered whether she was obliquely referring to our arrival—but she was the one who had insisted that we come.

'No.' Patrick set down his glass so heavily I expected it to crack. His lips tightened, his eyes looked more haunted than ever. 'I'll round up Luke. We ought to be going.' He went out of the back door, closing it with dangerous consideration.

'He isn't well,' Celia said softly. It was almost an apology. 'I suppose—' she sighed deeply— 'you and the

kids might as well drop over later. You haven't seen our
place yet.'

'Not tonight, thank you.' I have had more heartfelt
invitations in my time. 'We're still awfully tired and
slightly jet-lagged. I think we'll have a quiet evening,
perhaps watch television for a bit—we haven't seen any
yet—and have an early night.'

'As you think best.' Celia brightened. 'Perhaps you can
come to dinner tomorrow night. Oh no—' She brightened
even more. 'It's the cookout at camp tomorrow night.
Perhaps—'

'There's plenty of time,' I reminded her. 'We have all
summer.'

'That's right.' The thought did not appear to cheer
her. 'So we have.'

After dinner, I slumped down on the sofa and played with
the television set, using the remote control gadget to
switch off sound, change channels and generally discover
what could be done with it. Errol, replete with more fish
than he had a right to expect, stretched out beside me
throbbing like an outboard motor.

'Would you like a glass of iced water, Mummy?' Tessa
asked solicitously. I had demonstrated the ice-making
unit and it was more popular than the television.

'All right, thank you.' Until the novelty wore off, it was
clearly going to keep them out of mischief. Actually, I
agreed with them; it *was* more interesting than the
television.

The telephone rang, jolting me upright. I heard giggles
and the rush of feet from the kitchen.

'I'll get it—' I called. This time it might be someone we
knew: Greg calling to suggest proper costume for
tomorrow's cookout; or Luke to speak to his cousins; but I
was still uneasy enough to wish to monitor the call.

'Hello—' I said cautiously.

'Well, hi there! I'm glad I caught you at home. I dropped round earlier, but you were out.' It was a female voice, unidentified, but apparently friendly.

'We went out with Celia and Patrick—' I relaxed a bit but remained cautious. 'They drove us around, we had lunch at Gino's Place and did a lot of shopping at the supermarket.'

'Well, swell! Are you going to be home tomorrow morning? I'll come round and see you then.'

'Excuse me—' It was becoming apparent that this could go on indefinitely and I would be landed with a still unidentified stranger on the doorstep in the morning. 'You obviously have the advantage. To whom am I speaking?'

'Oh, sorry. I'm Pixie Toller. A friend of Nancy's.'

'Oh yes—' Now I could place her. 'The elderberry brandy. And those delicious vanilla biscuits.'

'That's right!' She was pleased. 'Also the Welcome Wagon. I'll drive it round in the morning and get you off to a proper start in town. That's why I called. Not that I wouldn't have, anyway. Nancy is a very good friend of mine and I promised her I'd look after you.'

'I'll be delighted to meet you. Er, what's a Welcome Wagon?'

'Wait and see!' She laughed gaily and rang off.

I returned to the living-room in time to see that a news broadcast had started. A close-up of an urgent intelligent face mouthing words voicelessly was replaced by an action shot of firemen surrounding a burning building. I sat down and reactivated the sound.

'. . . DOWNTOWN BOSTON . . .' The words roared at me from the set with the urgency of the leaping flames. I adjusted the volume hastily.

'This is the fourteenth fire in Boston's business section in four months. That's a rate of nearly one a week. Other city centres throughout Massachusetts and the

surrounding New England states have been similarly
afflicted. In May, in Concord, New Hampshire, three
people lost their lives when—'

Another picture flashed on to the screen: a gutted ruin,
smoke still rising from the charred wooden crossbeams of
what had been a small shop. At the edge of the pavement
lay three ominous shapes shrouded in blankets.

Errol stirred uneasily. He gazed unblinkingly at the
screen, seemingly mesmerized by the fire and smoke. I
heard Timothy's voice in the hallway, then Tessa's. They
had apparently wearied at last of their game with the ice-
making equipment.

'. . . Deputy Fire Commissioner Francis X. Alton today
renewed his appeal to the public to come forward with
any information—'

A grave, harassed man looked out from the screen
obviously striving for eye-to-eye contact with the invisible
audience.

'If any of you knows of anything that might possibly be
helpful,' he said desperately, 'please contact us
immediately. If you think you have seen or heard
anything suspicious, we want to know about it. Don't be
afraid of wasting our time. Don't be afraid that your
information isn't important enough. Let us be the judge
of that. Any scrap of information added to the
information we already have might be the means of
bringing the perpetrators of these outrages to justice. We
will keep your name confidential. I appeal to you to come
forward—'

'Mummy—' Tessa was fretful and on the verge of tears.
'Mummy, the machine isn't doing the ice right any more.
It's gone all sloppy.'

'Maybe you've worn it out.' I wasn't surprised. 'It isn't
supposed to be non-stop toy. Let's give it a rest until
morning now. It's probably all worn out—and so are you.
It's time for bed.'

Errol stretched, considered, then leaped to the floor and marched purposefully to the door. For him, it was time for other things. He looked back at us and gave an impatient command, waiting for someone to come and let him out.

Automatically, I switched the television off first. The message emblazoned across the screen grew momentarily larger, then dwindled away as though receding into Time:

'Ring ARSONLINE . . .

'24 hours a day service . . .'

CHAPTER 6

It was hot . . . so hot. I tossed and turned, trying to find a cool spot on the bed, but the sheet grew hot as soon as I had rested on it for a moment and the spot I had deserted did not cool down fast enough to keep up with my restless churning. There was no escape anywhere. How would I get through the endless hours until morning?

It grew hotter still . . . my nostrils twitched suddenly. Was that smoke? Even as I asked myself the question, the room blurred at the edges, as though the smoke were already encroaching.

I struggled out of bed. Had we turned the television set off properly? Had the children overheated the refrigerator while playing with the ice-making gadget? Or were the woods behind the house alight?

The room was filled with smoke now. It had to be coming from inside the house. I could just make out the pale oblong of the doorway. I struggled towards it.

'*Mummy . . . Mummy . . .*' The voices were frightened and far away. '*Mummy . . .*'

'*I'm coming . . .*' I seemed to struggle without making

any progress. The smoke thickened by the second. The doorway was almost obscured. I was disorientated . . . lost . . . I could not reach the children . . .

'*Mummy . . . Mummy . . .*' And then they were there in the room with me, pressing against me, clinging to me. I realized with horror that I could see them so clearly because the doorway had burst into flames behind them. We could not get out that way.

We could not get out at all. We were trapped.

'*Rosemary . . .*' The warm familiar voice called to me. '*Rosemary . . . over here . . .*'

John was standing outside the window.

'*Oh, my darling!*' I rushed to him, herding the children before me. '*My darling, you're here!*'

'*Where else would I be when you needed me?*' His loving eyes met mine. We pantomimed a kiss to each other; the children were still between us, preventing physical contact.

'*Now . . .*' John was immediately practical. '*Pass the children out to me and I'll lower them to the ground . . . Tessa first . . .*'

'*All right . . .*' I picked Tessa up and swung her over the window sill. '*Be careful of her arm . . .*'

'*Her arm?*' He frowned down at the plaster cast. '*What's the matter with it?*'

'*It's broken . . .*' Something was wrong. The smoke was curling through the window, swirling around John, beginning to obscure his outline.

'*When did that happen?*' He was still frowning.

'*Soon after . . .*' My voice faltered. I did not want to finish the sentence. But his eyes held mine with frowning, loving concern.

'*When . . . ?*' he insisted.

'*Soon after . . . you died . . .*' He was shrouded in smoke now. I could scarcely see him. He was fading away.

'*No! No!*' I could not let him go. I swept Timothy and

Tessa aside, reaching out towards him. '*They told me you were dead—but it was a lie. Some terrible mistake. You're here now. You're with us again. You're alive!*'

'No, Rosemary . . .' He spoke sadly, softly. I could scarcely hear him. I could scarcely see him. He was dissolving into the smoke.

'No, Rosemary, I'm dead.'

In the distance, there was a dull hollow thud, like a coffin lid falling.

I awoke trying to scream.

For a terrible moment, I thought I *had* screamed. Had I wakened the children? I caught my breath and listened.

Silence.

The ache in my throat was evidence of the force with which the scream had tried to tear loose. Somewhere in my mind, I was still screaming.

I took a deep breath and a sob escaped me. I swallowed hard. That would never do. Not yet.

I crept from the room and down the hallway, the terrors of the nightmare still gripping me. I looked for flickers of flame. I sniffed for smoke. I would not let myself think of John.

I stood outside Timothy's room, and then Tessa's, for a long time. They were sleeping peacefully although every once in a while a whimper escaped one of them. I wondered what sort of dreams they were having.

Downstairs, the television set was silent—and safe. No sparks, no smoke. In the kitchen, the refrigerator hummed comfortably, an occasional tinkle of shifting ice telling that it was renewing itself for the coming day. The woods outside were dark and cool, rustling in the pre-dawn wind that had sprung up.

Upstairs again, I checked on the children once more. Still sleeping, still undisturbed. I must not disturb them now.

I went into the bathroom. If they woke, they must hear only the familiar soothing sound of running water.

And yet the dream had not been entirely bad. For those brief moments, John had been there. Loving and supportive, when I needed him . . .

'*Where else would I be?*'

I turned on the shower and, standing beside it, sobbed myself into exhaustion.

When I awoke the second time, the sun was shining. I heard the children stirring downstairs. The children . . . there *was* a reason to get up and go on . . .

For a moment I closed my eyes, fighting off the phantoms of the night. It was morning. Pixie Toller was coming round with something called the Welcome Wagon. Tonight we were invited to the cookout at Camp Mohigonquin. There were two focal points of the day. It was more than some days had . . .

I shut off my mind, got up and dressed. Tessa, still in her nightie, looked up as I entered the kitchen.

'Errol isn't here,' she worried. 'He didn't come home last night.'

'That's all right.' I wasn't surprised. 'He'll be along later. Why don't you run upstairs and get dressed now? We have a new friend coming to see us soon. You want to look nice, don't you?'

'*I'm* dressed,' Timothy pointed out as Tessa darted away.

'Then you'd better sit down and have your breakfast—' I shook cornflakes into the waiting bowls— 'before Errol comes along and steals it again.'

We had just finished eating when I heard the sound of a car drawing up outside and then a horn played the opening bars of the *Habañera*.

'That must be Pixie Toller,' I guessed. It sounded like the sort of horn someone called Pixie would have. We went out to greet her.

'Oh, *Mummy!*' Tessa exclaimed.

'Crumbs!' Timothy said.

Even I binked twice.

Pixie Toller couldn't really be eight feet tall but, at first sight, she looked it. And she was carrying a beribboned wicker basket that looked even taller than she did.

'Hello! Hello! Hello—and welcome!' She bounded up the steps and set the basket down before us. Now she seemed to have shrunk to a mere seven feet.

'I just *love* your cute little accent!' she gushed on. 'Even Celia can't talk like that any more—she's been here too long. Do you think you could teach it to me? I would *adore* to pass as English!'

The mind boggled. She was wearing some sort of glittering jumpsuit. From a headband sprouted shimmering antennæ which quivered with every movement of her head. Her dark glasses were rimmed with mirror fragments, reflecting distorted images of ourselves as we stared at her.

Behind her, a shooting brake—station wagon, I must learn to say—was painted in iridescent colours vaguely reminiscent of the psychedelic phase of Flower Childhood and blazoned with the legend WELCOME WAGON in Gothic script.

She bent to make some rearrangement of the flowers spilling out of the wicker basket and, before I could do anything to avert it, Tessa stuck out a tentative forefinger and poked at one shimmering antenna.

'Do you like it?' Pixie Toller straightened with an eager smile and Tessa shrank back. 'It's the latest fashion—Harper's Bizarre! That's a joke—' she explained to Tessa's puzzled frown. 'It's all right to laugh. You're supposed to.'

For an uncertain moment Tessa was poised between laughter and tears, then the laughter won. I realized, as the peals of merriment rang out, that I had not heard her laugh like that since John died.

I looked at Pixie Toller with gratitude, prepared to forgive her any eccentricity in return for the gift of laughter she had bestowed on my daughter. There was more to Pixie Toller than was apparent on the surface.

Timothy was chuckling. I looked from one child to the other and felt a smile curving my own lips.

'That's better,' Pixie said. 'And you haven't even seen what I've brought you yet!' She began pulling parcels out from among the flowers in the basket.

'Hanson's Hardware feels that anyone can always use another egg poacher—' She thrust at me a circular package from which protuded a black handle surmounted by a bow. 'I'm not supposed to mention that Old Man Hanson overbought on the item a couple of years ago and hasn't been able to unload them since. But if you need anything else in the hardware line, he has a good stock at reasonable prices.

'A bottle of California white wine and a large cream soda from Cut-Price Liquors—' She plonked them at my feet. 'A pound of frozen pork chops from the Mini-Market; three frozen TV dinners from the Supermarket; a quart of chocolate chip ice cream from Daly's Drugstore. The vegetable assortment—zucchini squash, tomatoes, string beans and scallions—is from the Roadside Vegetable Shop; the boxes of blueberries, raspberries and loganberries are from—'

'Stop!' I cried, as the cornucopia emptied at my feet, threatening to engulf me. 'What *is* all this?'

'It's your Welcome Wagon welcome—' Pixie straightened up and beamed at me. 'Don't you have it in England?'

'No,' I said faintly. Whatever it was, I certainly had seen nothing like it before. 'What's it all about?'

'It's the welcome from your friendly local merchants to

newcomers moving into the area,' Pixie explained. 'They all—well, most of them—provide samples of their wares free of charge as an introduction, in the hope that you'll patronize them when you go shopping.

'Oh, it pays off—' she assured me. 'They wouldn't do it, otherwise. It's all marked down to goodwill and it works. You may not have it over there, but it's big business here. This time of the year, it's practically a full-time job for me, driving around to all the summer cottages and welcoming visitors. You see, there are a lot of summer lets up in the hills that are just for two or three weeks at a time. You're one of the very few who are going to be here for the whole summer.'

'I hadn't thought of it that way,' I equivocated. I hadn't thought of it at all. I looked down at the pile at my feet. 'Shouldn't we get this stuff into the freezer before it defrosts?'

'No hurry,' Pixie said casually. 'The insulated bags will keep it for another couple of hours yet. Let me foist upon you the rest of the bounty—' She produced a sheaf of envelopes from the bottom of the basket and began pushing them into my unresisting hands.

'Free tickets to the Edgemarsh Movie Palace—they're running a special Disney Season starting in July. Then—' another envelope—'a free dinner at Gino's Place. It's usually for two, but since there's only one of you and two children who'll order from the childrens' menu, you'll all get a free dinner—'

'But we've already been to Gino's Place,' I protested. 'Celia and Patrick took us yesterday.'

'That has nothing to do with it. You're entitled to a free dinner in your own right. Just give them this voucher as you order.'

'*Prr-yee-ow* . . ." Errol staggered out of the shrubbery at the edge of the lawn, wove his way across it, and lurched up the steps to collapse at my feet. His eyes closed and he lay there unmoving.

'Mummy!' Tessa shrieked. 'Mummy—he's dead! He went away where we couldn't see him—and he came back dead!' She burst into tears.

'Mum—' Timothy was shaken, fighting back tears himself. 'Mum, he isn't really dead—is he?'

'Dead tired,' Pixie said practically. She prodded Errol with the toe of her sandal. He twitched and, after a long moment, sent out a rough perfunctory purr. 'The old reprobate!'

'Dead tired—but happy,' I agreed. How very different from the home life of our own dear Esmond. At some point I was going to have to do some explaining to the children—but I didn't feel up to it right now. I sent Pixie a helpless glance.

'Errol's fine,' she said. 'Just move him into the shade—' She suited the action to the words; he gave one final purr and went silent again. 'Now why don't we have some of this delicious cream soda? We'll need glasses and lots of ice—'

'I'll get it!' both children shouted at once. They dived for the kitchen.

I looked after Tessa anxiously. Her reaction had betrayed fears lurking deep in her mind. I could understand, but how could I teach her that people—or pets—could not be shut up in little boxes and stored away in a safe place until their presence was required? That they must be allowed to live their own lives—even though they might encounter danger? Had I learned the lesson yet myself? Why was I fighting the idea of enrolling the children as day campers at Camp Mohigonquin? Hadn't we all learned that there was no real safety anywhere? *In the midst of life* . . .

'You're right,' Pixie said shrewdly, diagnosing—correctly—that I needed distraction myself. 'It's time we got all this frozen stuff into the freezer.' She stooped and began gathering it up. "This is no weather to leave it lying around.'

I picked up the remaining items when her arms were full and led the way into the kitchen. The children had already filled four tumblers to the brim with ice and pounced on the bottle of cream soda, although the glasses seemed too full of ice to allow room for much liquid to be added.

'I *like* Welcome Wagons—' Timothy wrestled with the bottle cap. 'Why don't we have them in England?'

'English shopkeepers hate to give anything away,' Pixie answered for me. 'I've heard Celia say so often enough. They either figure they've got a captive clientele or they just don't care. Patrick says they've never heard of merchandising or salesmanship.'

'They may have heard of them—they just don't believe in them.' Now that I was getting a demonstration of American methods, I could understand Patrick's point of view.

'Thank you, honey.' Pixie accepted the glass Tessa held out to her. 'That will sure hit the spot. I must admit I'm beginning to feel the heat.' She sighed wearily. 'It's been going on for weeks—and the nights aren't cooling down the way they used to. Even when we had a couple of thunderstorms, they didn't clear the air.'

'I'm hot, too,' Tessa said.

'Everybody is.' Pixie held the icy glass up against one temple and rolled it slowly across her forehead, then back again.

Tessa watched with fascination and, a moment later, casually copied the gesture. Her fringe was in the way, though, and the water beads on the outside of the glass combined with her perspiration to leave damp tendrils straggling down into her eyes.

'You ought to be wearing your hair off your face in this weather,' Pixie advised. 'It's too hot for bangs.'

I kept silent; it was something I had not dared suggest
to Tessa. However, she was willing to accept it from a
stranger. She nodded agreement and swept her fringe to
one side; it still covered half her forehead.

'Here, this is what you need—' Pixie removed her
headband. 'It may not be quite your style, but it will hold
your hair back until you can get something you like
better.' She tucked Tessa's fringe under the headband
and adjusted it. Mercifully she didn't comment on the
unveiled widow's peak.

'We can snap off the thingamabobs, if you want—' she
offered.

'No, thank you, I like them.' Tessa turned to me, eyes
shining. 'May I wear it tonight, Mummy? Please?'

'Of course,' I said and, to Pixie, 'Thank you.'

'Tonight . . .' Pixie gazed out of the window
thoughtfully. 'You're going to the cookout at camp, Celia
tells me.'

'That's right.' For the first time, there had been a
certain reserve in her tone. 'Why?'

'Oh, nothing. I suppose Greg knows what he's doing,
but I'm surprised he's still having cookouts. I wouldn't
think it was quite safe with the woods so dry. He'll have to
watch where every spark flies—'

'Perhaps we ought not to go—'

The children immediately chorused protest.

'Oh, I'm sure it will be all right,' Pixie said. 'Greg's
careful. In fact, you'd better go, if you want to see a
proper cookout. By this time next week, the Park Rangers
may have outlawed camp fires in the woods. I'm surprised
they haven't already, but I suppose they're trying to hold
off until after the Fourth of July. It wouldn't be the same
without the big bonfire and fireworks.'

'There seem to be a lot of fires around,' I said uneasily.
'I was watching television last night and—'

'Oh, it's turning into a major industry.' Pixie laughed

cheerfully. 'The one boom industry the recession has produced. It's saved a lot of small businesses.'

'Saved?'

'Sure. They all carry fire insurance, perhaps more than they need. Then, if the business looks like failing, they have a quiet talk with their friendly neighbourhood Torch and then make arrangements to be far, far away—preferably in the company of a dozen unimpeachable witnesses—on the night the business goes up. Everybody knows it's going on. It's just awfully hard to prove—unless you can catch the Torch in the act.'

'That's appalling!'

'Depends on how you look at it.' She shrugged. 'It's been worse. In the nineteen-thirties Depression a lot of men committed suicide so that their families would get the insurance money and be able to survive. I can sympathize with the ones who'd rather cash in on their fire insurance—even it does mean gaol if they're caught.'

'Is that what it's all about? I mean, ARSONLINE and the appeals from the police—?'

'Well, sure. Even without the insurance angle, it's dangerous. Your Torch is a professional, starting fires for money. The problem is, he can set off the carbon copy nuts, the firebugs, who do it because they like to see the fire engines or—' She glanced at the children and lowered her voice meaningfully. 'Or for *kicks*. They're the dangerous ones. They don't care what they set alight. An empty building, an automobile, somebody's home—it's all one to them. They aren't fussy, either, about making sure the place is unoccupied.'

I shivered. Last night's nightmare suddenly had deeper import than I had thought.

'Oh, you don't have to worry here,' Pixie said lightly. 'Those things are just happening down in the cities. This is really a very law-abiding neck of the woods.'

CHAPTER 7

Celia picked us up and drove us to Camp Mohigonquin, but dropped us at the gate.

'Luke's already there,' she said. 'I won't come in. I can't stay. I've made arrangements with Greg, either he or Lois will drive you home.'

'But—'

'I *can't* stay,' she repeated peevishly. 'You've *seen* Patrick. He needs a quiet evening, just the two of us. That's why I sent Luke on ahead—with permission to stay overnight.'

'Celia—' The children had tumbled out of the car and were walking up the path. 'Celia, what *is* the matter with Patrick? Is it . . . serious?'

'Serious enough.' She laughed shortly. 'But not in the way you mean. They call it Executive Burnout. He went too far, too fast. He sort of . . . couldn't keep up with himself. And he couldn't slow down, because the pressure never let up. The younger people are crowding along, pushing, trying to take over. It's not quite a nervous breakdown—but it's not far off. It happens to a lot of them. That's why they've got a name for the syndrome now.'

She studied the sandy path between the pine trees, avoiding my eyes. 'Even the Indians knew about it. They had better ways of handling it than we have. In the old days, after an Indian made a long journey, he retired to a hogan for a few days when he reached his destination. Just to sit quietly and wait for his soul to catch up with him. That's what Patrick needs now. Time for his soul to catch up with him.'

'Yes,' I said. Patrick looked as though he needed a lot more than that.

'We've saved you seats in front.' Luke led us through a triple circle of children of assorted ages who were sitting cross-legged around the fire and signing some incomprehensible song about the joys of Camp Mohigonquin. 'The cushion is yours,' he told me thoughtfully.

I perched sidesaddle on the cushion and steadied Tessa as she lowered herself to the ground. The boys promptly dropped into the obligatory cross-legged position and gazed fervently at the two adults who were occupied in opening large packets of frankfurters.

'Here's yours—' Luke shook out three long willowy sticks sharpened to a stake-point at the thin end, from a pile by his side. I had assumed that they were being kept there to replenish the campfire when needed, but apparently I was wrong. I noticed now that each child was hopefully clutching a similar stick or thin bough.

'Mrs Blake—' Greg materialized before me. 'Since you're sort of the Guest of Honor tonight—' he began threading frankfurters on to my stick—'you get first whack over the campfire.'

'Wait a minute,' I protested. 'If I'm supposed to eat all those, I can't possibly—'

'Oh?' He looked surprised; obviously he was accustomed to more robust appetites. 'But there's only three.'

'Don't worry—' Dexter leaned close and whispered. 'I'll eat anything you can't manage.' His eyes gleamed in the firelight.

'Well, all right,' I said weakly to Greg. 'But three is *quite* enough.' Dexter nudged me reprovingly.

Lois is doing the rolls,' Greg explained. 'We coat them with a low-cal spread. And Luke will go round with the mustard and relish. You don't have to cook the hot dogs all at once,' he added, 'But it's better to get them and hold on to them before the ravening hordes—' he indicated the children behind us with a sweep of his hand—'descend.'

'Ah yes.' I could appreciate that. Already I seemed to feel hot eager eyes greedily devouring the sausages at the end of my stick.

'And here's yours—' Greg lavished three hot dogs each on Tessa's and Timothy's sticks before turning to Dexter.

'And you, ol' buddy—just to keep us company, huh?'

I began to feel a sneaking sympathy for Dexter. Greg placed a single hot dog on the end of his stick. It must have been the smallest thinnest hot dog in the entire package. Even Errol would have sneered at it.

'Sure, Greg,' Dexter said complacently. 'Whatever you say.'

Greg glanced at him sharply, with justifiable suspicion, but was sidetracked when the young woman strolled over to join us. She was wearing jeans and a white T-shirt with a message emblazoned in green across the front: 'You've got to kiss a lot of ugly frogs before you find a Prince.' Greg looked at her with approval.

'You haven't met Lois yet, have you, Mrs Blake?' Greg presented her to me. 'Lois is our Registered Nurse, Camp Counsellor, Crafts Instructor and—'

'And I also double at cooking on cookout nights,' Lois finished for him. 'Hi there, I'm glad to meet you.' She shook hands all around. 'Welcome to Camp Mohigonquin—I know you're going to like it here.'

'I already do!' Timothy said unreservedly. He and Luke had settled down to a whispered conversation interrupted by asides to some of the other boys. It looked as though Timothy would settle in well.

Tessa was silent. She shrank back against me when Lois released her hand. She gazed thoughtfully into the campfire, while the fingers of her freed hand scrabbled at the plaster cast making little scratching noises.

'Itching means it's getting better,' Lois said sympathetically, 'but it's awful, I know. Wait a minute—' She disappeared into one of the buildings and re-emerged with a long steel knitting needle.

'Here.' She leaned over to give it to Tessa. A green jade frog swung from a chain around her neck, further reinforcing the sentiment of her T-shirt, as she did so. 'That ought to slide into your cast and let you have a good scratch. Don't overdo it, though, you don't want to break the skin.'

'Thank you,' Tessa murmured shyly. She slid the knitting needle between her arm and the cast and moved it around tentatively. A slow smile spread across her face.

'That's better,' Lois said. 'You keep that until the cast comes off. It will make you a bit more comfortable.'

'They're waiting for you, Mrs Blake,' Greg reminded me. 'If you'd like to kick off now. Just hold your hot dogs over the fire—not too low.'

I duly crouched forward and held my hot dogs above the flames at what I judged to be a suitable distance. I was aware that Lois had moved away and begun splitting and spreading the long soft rolls in readiness to receive the hot dogs. After a moment, urged by Greg, Tessa crept forward and held her stick over the fire, then Timothy did the same. We all concentrated, turning the hot dogs occasionally, trying to ensure that they didn't drop off the sticks and into the fire.

The skins of the hot dogs began to char, a delicious odour filled the air. Abruptly, the skin split on one of mine, releasing a stream of sizzling fat into the campfire, sending a shower of sparks leaping upwards.

'Okay, you're done,' Greg said. 'Move back and sit down and let the next shift take over.'

We got out of the way quickly as the children behind us surged forward, thrusting sticks over the fire, some of them deliberately knocking against other sticks as though jousting to knock each other's frankfurters into the flames.

'Okay, you kids, settle down!' Greg called out. 'No wasting food, you know the rules. If you can't behave, you can go straight to bed without supper.'

A chorus of jeers and catcalls answered him, but it was noticeable that the pushing stopped and the hot dogs were held at reasonable distances from each other.

'Here you are.' Lois appeared with the rolls and paper plates. Luke heaped mustard and piccalilli on one side of the plates and dispensed plastic knives before moving off.

As soon as Lois disappeared, so did two of the hot dogs on my plate. Dexter's cheeks bulged like a chipmunk's at harvest time and he was already eyeing Tessa's surplus hot dogs.

I was more worried about all those sparks I had caused. They still seemed to be moving about in the woods. I watched anxiously lest they ignite some of the dry pine needles and cones covering the ground.

'What's the matter?' Greg's eyes had followed my anxious gaze.

'The sparks—they don't seem to be dying down. They might start a fire—'

'No way!' Greg's hearty laugh was at my expense. 'Those aren't sparks—they're fireflies. The woods are full of them. They can't do any harm. Most people think they're kind of pretty.'

'So they are.' Reassured, I could admire them myself. 'I'm afraid I was over-reacting. The television last night—' I could not mention the dream.

' 'S'aw'ri'—' Dexter swallowed and tried again. 'Don't worry, Mrs Blake. You think this could start a forest fire? Just wait until you see our Fourth of July celebrations!'

The last marshmallows were toasted and the sticky

glutinous mass consumed; the fire died to embers; the final hymn of praise to Camp Mohigonquin rang out on the still night air and the children dispersed to their dormitories.

Greg poured the remains of the bucket of hot chocolate on to the embers, then stamped them into the earth for good measure.

'Okay—' Greg loomed over me; the teeth had an almost phosphorescent glow in the moonlight. 'Let's go.'

'Where's Luke?' I looked around uneasily. Suddenly we were suspended in space in an unfamiliar world; we might have slipped backward in time into an earlier century. The trees whispered an ancient secret language; a cloud shadowed the moon, darkening our clearing, obscuring the path back to civilization. There were shadows everywhere.

Tessa was asleep. Timothy was nowhere in sight; he had disappeared at about the same time his cousin had. *I was alone, unprotected, vulnerable. What was I doing here? Why had I come? What was the sense of it all?*

'Luke won't be coming. He's got permission to stay here overnight. He and Dexter are working on a project for the Fourth of July Horribles Parade next week. They want to get an early start in the morning.'

Expertly, Greg swung two fingers into the sides of his mouth and whistled sharply, then picked up Tessa and walked towards the path to the gate. Before he reached the edge of the clearing, Timothy appeared, followed by Luke and Dexter. They indulged in some parting words, then Timothy fell into step beside me while Greg led the way down the path.

'Dexter says there'll be a place for me in camp on Monday,' Timothy informed me.

'That's right,' Greg said. 'We'll fit you in somewhere.'

'We can, can't we, Mum?' Timothy asked anxiously. 'Luke and Dexter said I can help them with their costumes if I come.'

'You don't have to decide this minute,' Greg said quickly as I hesitated. 'I don't want to crowd you.'

'Timothy can, certainly,' I agreed slowly. 'But I'm not so sure it would be the best thing for Tessa. Perhaps later, after the cast comes off. I'm afraid she couldn't keep up with the others right now.'

'We'd keep an eye on her, of course,' Greg said, 'but you're probably right. She'd want to go swimming and join in the other activities. It wouldn't be much fun for poor little Tessa to just stand around on the sidelines.'

Recognizing her name, Tessa stirred in her sleep. Her head moved on his shoulder and she gave a drowsy little murmur of contentment. She lifted her head, her eyes opened and she looked up at Greg's face.

Suddenly she screamed, burst into tears, and began fighting to get down.

'Hey, take it easy!' Greg let her slide to the ground and looked at me in dismay. 'I know it's not the greatest face in the world—but this is the first time it's got *that* reaction.'

'Her father used to carry her when she fell asleep,' I explained. 'She must have thought—' I knew all about such awakenings. 'When she saw it was a stranger—' My voice began to shake and I broke off.

'Sure,' Greg said quickly. 'Sure, I understand. Poor little kid. It's rough—rough on all of you. I'm sorry, Mrs Blake.'

I nodded, still unable to trust myself to speak. Timothy had put his arm around Tessa's shoulders and was steadying her. She kept on crying.

We had reached the small car park just inside the camp gates. Greg opened the car door for us and we drove back to Cranberry Lane in silence.

CHAPTER 8

Luke and Dexter were already in the car when Celia
drove up to collect us just before noon. Timothy leaped
into the back seat with them and they were immediately
deep in muttered conversation. Tessa slid into the front
seat between Celia and myself. There were only two seat-
belts, but there was not yet a law in America that said you
had to wear them and I had noticed that Celia never
bothered about hers.

Besides, what did it really matter? The seat-belt hadn't
saved John.

Celia seemed preoccupied throughout the drive. After
a couple of abortive attempts at conversation, I gave up
and contented myself with simple comments on the sights
along the way. She replied with equally simple assenting
noises. Only once did she show any animation.

A long gleaming station wagon swept past us on the
other side of the road. The occupants raised their hands
in greeting as they passed. Celia flashed them a bright
smile, but her hands tightened on the steering-wheel until
her knuckles turned white.

'Those silly people must be awfully hot,' Tessa
observed. 'They're driving with the windows closed.'

'Don't worry about *them*—' Celia gave a short harsh
laugh. 'That's the very latest model station
wagon—they're air-conditioned.

'You'll meet them sooner or later.' She flashed me that
same bright insincere smile. 'Viv and Hank Singleton.
They're our local antique dealers. That's why they can
afford such an expensive station wagon. They use it for
transporting the pieces they pick up—so it comes off their
income tax as a business expense. You'll like them,

though. They're very nice people, really.'

'I'm sure I'll like them,' I said, wondering if anyone that nice needed the qualifying afterthoughts.

However, it was the most expansive Celia had been so far and I hoped for more information or local gossip.

My hopes were dashed. Celia retreated into her former silence, lit another cigarette and concentrated on the road, which needed little or no concentration. Traffic was light to the point of non-existence. The Singletons' was the only other vehicle we encountered.

With a faint sigh of resignation, Celia pulled up before the house so familiar to me from all the proud photographs she had sent over.

That had been a long time ago—several years now. The house was recognizably the same, but a faint air of shabbiness had settled over it. The paint no longer gleamed brightly; the shrubbery around the house was ragged; even the window-panes seemed dulled.

'I suppose—' Celia sighed again—'you'd better come in.'

Luke, Dexter and Timothy were already tumbling up the path. Tessa and I followed more slowly, while Celia took her time over locking the car.

Patrick was standing in the hallway waiting to welcome us. His condition seemed to have deteriorated in just the short time since we had last seen him. The circles under his eyes were darker and more pronounced; there was a faint tremor in his hand as he patted Tessa's shoulder.

Tessa caught it, too. She looked up at me with sudden fear in her eyes. She had learned too well the lesson of the shortness of life, the swiftness with which someone could be swept away.

'I thought we'd have chicken salad as it's so hot.' Celia came up quickly, as though to distract us from awkward thoughts and, possibly, inquiries. 'Outside on the patio. It's usually a bit cooler out there.'

'Not that it's cool anywhere, these days.' Patrick seemed vaguely puzzled at the speed with which Celia led us through the house and out on to the flagstone-paved patio at the side.

Despite the speed. I had time to notice the wallpaper was starting to peel away at the foot of the stairs, the cobweb in the corner of the ceiling, the frayed edges of the stair carpet. This, in Celia's house! Celia, who had always been so houseproud.

There was something else wrong about the house. I could not put my finger on it, but it added to my uneasiness.

'Now, isn't this better? You sit there—' Celia indicated a plastic lounger—'and Patrick will go and get us some drinks.' She raised her voice. 'Patrick will get us drinks.'

'Oh yes, sure.' Patrick came out of his trance. He had been leaning against the doorframe staring unseeingly into space. 'Right away.' He stumbled blindly into the house.

'Oh dear. I think I'd better . . .' Celia let her thought trail off and turned and followed him, a look of deep concern on her face.

'*You* sit down,' I told Tessa. 'I'll be right back.'

Patrick's study seemed gloomier and even more un-inviting than it had when I had simply passed through it. Two doors stood open on the far side, giving no indication of what might lie beyond them. I hesitated but could hear no sound of footsteps or voices to guide me in the right direction. Celia and Patrick might have vanished off the face of the earth.

For that matter, there was no trace of the boys, either. The house seemed to have swallowed up everyone.

I started towards the door I thought I remembered. If I could find the hallway again, I ought to be able to find my way to the kitchen.

It was the wrong door. I seemed to be in the sort of cul-de-sac one used as a box room. At one time, Celia might have intended it as a sewing-room, but semed to have abandoned the idea. An adjustable dressmaker's dummy stood by the window. It was small, but still a size or two larger than Celia was right now. When had she lost all that weight?

An end table with a broken leg and splintery-looking rocking-chair jostled together with an ironing board at the far end of the room. At some point, a washing-machine and spin drier had been added. A shabby wicker basket was filled to overflowing with limp clothing which had seen better days. Dark patches on the wallpaper betrayed that pictures had once hung there when the room had been used for better purposes in a previous incarnation.

If it were mine, I would have used it as a morning room. It could still be pulled back into some sort of ordered charm despite its dispirited appearance.

But it was Celia's problem, not mine, and she would not be pleased if she returned and caught me mentally rearranging one of the shabbier rooms in the house.

I backed out hastily, tried the other door and found myself in the hallway. Celia had sent me a picture of the long, lovely hallway to show me where she had placed the Pembroke table they had bought on their first trip to England before Luke's birth. They had gone on a buying spree in the antique shops to furnish their new house with English heirlooms.

John and I had been aghast at the prices they had paid without a quibble, not to mention the cost of shipping things back to the States. But time and inflation had soon taught us that what had seemed mad extravagance had merely been clever buying and wise investment.

Celia had sent triumphant photographs of the pieces *in situ* throughout the house: the carriage clock on the living-room mantelpiece; the Davenport desk in the corner of the living-room; the Pembroke table in the front hall just below the curve of the stairs—

The Pembroke table was missing. That was what had registered subconsciously as I had negotiated the hallway earlier, causing my initial uneasiness.

I looked around, not really expecting to find that it had been moved elsewhere. Celia had enthused too emphatically over the absolute perfection of every placement. Each piece seemed to her to have been designed for the exact location she had chosen and she could visualize no other spot for it. She was not a person who constantly rearranged her furniture. She furnished for the ages—at least, that was what she had intended when buying the furniture.

There had been one of many later acquisitions, a Chinese Chippendale mirror, above the table. Again, a dark oblong patch on the fading wallpaper gave witness to radical changes in the original decor.

It wasn't any of my business. With a mental shake of my head, I tried to dismiss what appeared to be a long-term problem and concentrate on the immediate question.

Where had Celia and Patrick gone? And where was the kitchen?

I turned towards the back of the house, moving silently. I felt instinctively that it was not for me to disturb the deep hush of this house. I ignored doors on either side of the hallway, holding firmly to the theory that kitchens were usually at the rear of the house.

The end of the hallway loomed ahead, with a door promisingly ajar and the murmur of voices beyond the door. I hurried towards it. Just as I was about to push it open and call out a greeting, something in the tone of Celia's voice stopped me cold.

The door silently swung farther open under my touch and revealed a scene no one was meant to see.

Patrick was clinging to Celia, face hidden in her

bosom, shaking with silent sobs. Celia cradled him in her arms, staring over his head with a look of burning desperation.

'Please, Patrick—' she was pleading. 'You promised me this summer. Please, please, darling, hold on. Until October. At least, September. Oh, please . . .' her voice broke. 'Please let me have this one last summer . . .'

I was out of breath when I reached the patio, but I had escaped unseen. Celia and Patrick need never know I had been there, if only I could keep from betraying my guiltily-acquired knowledge.

No wonder Celia had been so anxious for me to come over. It looked as though she were going to need me more than I needed her. The worst shock of my widowhood was over—hers was still to come. Or was the shock of fore-knowledge worse than the sudden appalling desolation that had befallen me? What would have been the difference if John and I had known what was to come and been able to discuss it and try to strengthen each other to face it?

'Mummy?' Tessa's small face was puckered with anxiety. 'Mummy, are you all right?'

'Yes, darling, I'm fine.' I saw, with relief, that the boys had returned from their mysterious mission. Of course, nothing could have happened to them in the short time they had been gone. And yet . . .

'Where have you been?' I rounded on poor Timothy with more vehemence than I had intended. 'What do you mean by running off like that?'

'I'm sorry.' Timothy answered the thought, not the question, while the other two boys looked puzzled. They had not yet had that brush with the ultimate which would decipher adult fears and incomphrehensible behaviour for them. 'I didn't know we were going to be gone so long, or I'd have told you. We've been adding to the bonfire down at the lake.'

'We were only just down there—' Dexter waved an arm towards a towering ramshackle structure visible at the edge of the lake about half a mile away. 'You could have seen us—if you'd looked.'

I had been looking elsewhere.

'Isn't it a super bonfire?' Timothy came to my rescue. 'They do theirs now—instead of Guy Fawkes Night—with fireworks and everything.'

'We don't have Guy Fawkes Night,' Luke said. 'This is for the Fourth of July.'

'Yeah,' Dexter said. 'That's when we threw the British out. We've been celebrating it ever since.'

'That isn't very polite,' Tessa reproved him primly. '*We're* English.'

'Oh, I don't mean you,' Dexter said. 'I mean history.'

'It's a splendid bonfire,' I intervened hastily. 'But what's that you've got on top instead of a Guy? It looks like a shed—or was it a tree house?'

'It's old man Peterson's privy,' Luke said. 'We've been after it for years and we've finally got it. Good thing, too, there aren't many left around these parts. I suppose, by the time I'm grown up, there won't be any at all and we'll have to find something else to top the pile.'

'It's good and old!' Dexter's eyes gleamed enthusiastically. 'It ought to go up like nobody's business! Some of them shoot off as many sparks as a rocket when the wood is that old and dry.' He sounded quite expert on the subject.

'Not too many sparks, I hope.' I looked around uneasily; you could smell the heat in the air, leaves rustled drily in the warm wind, the woods were fast approaching the tinderbox stage. 'If we haven't had some rain by then, it could be dangerous.'

'Don't worry,' Luke said easily. 'The Fire Department always keeps an engine standing by. When it's like this, they wet down the area all around the bonfire before they even let us light it.'

'Yeah—' The thought made Dexter morose. 'Bunch of old killjoys.'

'Oh, come now,' I said. 'You wouldn't want the whole town to go up in flames, would you?'

'Wouldn't I?' His eyes gleamed dangerously. 'This whole town is nothing but one big gaolhouse—it deserves to burn down.'

'Aw, Dex, it isn't that bad,' Luke protested.

'Maybe not for *you*—' Dexter broke off, looking over my shoulder. His features abruptly rearranged themselves into a welcoming smile; he looked a different person. 'Let me give you a hand with that, Mrs Meadows.'

'Thank you, Dexter.' Celia smiled as Dexter came forward to grasp the front of the three-tiered Victorian rosewood tea-trolley and help her ease it over the threshold. She was using her crystal punchbowl as a salad bowl, a silver-topped claret jug was filled with lemonade, cakes were piled high on a Wedgwood plate.

I was glad to see that she still had some of her treasured antiques. Her friendly local antique dealers hadn't got their hands on everything, then. Not yet.

I looked at Celia searchingly in the light of my new knowledge, but her mask was back in place. Her face was untroubled, the very slight frown of concentration clearing as she and Dexter coaxed the tea-trolley over the threshold without mishap.

'That looks great, Mrs Meadows,' Dexter approved. 'Just great.'

'Here we are.' Patrick appeared in the doorway bearing a straw bread basket lined with a gleaming white linen table napkin. When he turned back the folds to offer me a corn muffin, a cloud of fragrant steam rose from the depths.

His face, also, was untroubled. Well, as untroubled as I

had yet seen it. Nothing was going to erase those deeply-etched lines around his mouth and eyes; they were there to stay, no matter what might happen in the future.

If he had a future. I averted my eyes, lest he read the thought in them.

'I saw Dr Peterson driving through town this morning,' he informed me. 'That's Jonah's nephew. He's going to be living at the Peterson place for the summer, so he'll be your nearest neighbour. I'm glad of that. He could be very useful to you.'

'Oh, I shouldn't think we'd need to call on him,' I said. 'Tessa's arm seems to be mending well. Anyway, Nancy left a different doctor's name to be called in case of emergency.'

'He's a Doctor of Literature—' Celia laughed for the first time—'not medicine. He's here to work on a book of local history. In any case, Nancy and Arnold never met him. He's only been up here for the odd weekend until term ended. They've been rushing around so much getting ready to leave, we've scarcely seen them ourselves. We met Noah because Jonah brought him over to introduce him and explain he was taking over the house for the summer. Jonah always disappears into the mountains for the summer himself. But we'll have Noah over sometime so that you can meet him. I think you'll like him.'

'Fine,' I said. Celia would not understand that likes or dislikes did not matter. I was in some strange limbo where nothing seemed quite real and other people slid across my consciousness like shadows. I didn't feel real myself. I walked, I talked, I must be making the right responses to situations since no one seemed to notice that I was empty and hollow, a living ghost haunting a world that no longer concerned me.

'You'll like him,' Celia insisted. She frowned at me uneasily.

I nodded and dredged up a sympathetic smile. I was

afraid that it would not be long before Celia knew more
than she wanted to know about such feelings.

CHAPTER 9

He must have been lurking in the bushes when Celia
brought us home. Then he waited for her to drive away
and leave us. The sound of her car engine had hardly
faded into the distance when the front doorbell rang, a
sharp demanding peal.

It was late for anyone to be calling. Slightly alarmed, I
glanced at Tessa and Timothy. They were opening a tin
of cat food for Errol, who was twining around their
ankles, and did not appear to notice anything amiss in the
situation.

'Yes—?' I opened the door cautiously, wishing that
Nancy and Arnold were less trusting. They might have
taken the rudimentary precaution of having a chain on
their door. I did not recognize the dark male shape
looming before me. 'What is it?'

'What is it? I'll tell you what it is, lady—' He pushed
past me and stood foursquare in the hallway, scowling
and narrowing his eyes against the light.

'Now just a minute—' I protested.

'What it is, is—' He was snarling with fury. I backed
away. 'Your cat has knocked up my cat—and I want to
know what you're going to do about it!'

'Poor sweet.' Tessa had come to see what was
happening. 'Can't she get back to sleep again?'

'If there's one thing I can't stand—' the man turned his
contorted face to Tessa—'it's an insolent brat!'

'It isn't insolence—it's innocence!' I flew to Tessa's
defence, annoyed but no longer quite so frightened. It is
difficult to be afraid of a man—however large and bad-

tempered — who is tenderly cradling a gloriously beautiful picture-book cat in his arms. She appeared to be a long-haired Siamese with big blue perfectly round eyes which were watching us all with interest.

'Look at her' He gently stroked the cat's bulging sides. 'Just look at what your revolting monster has done to my poor little Pitti-Sing. That beast ought to be put down!'

Tessa pressed close to me and tugged at my skirt. I bent to her. 'I don't like that man, Mummy,' she whispered.

I wasn't exactly enamoured of him myself, but he appeared to have genuine cause for grievance.

'Put down!' he repeated. Tessa whimpered.

'That's out of the question,' I said firmly. 'Just because you can't keep your own cat under control, there's no need to take it out on Errol.'

'She's never out of my apartment in the city,' he said. 'I thought it was safe to let her enjoy the great outdoors up here. I didn't know that monster was prowling the woods, or I'd never have let her out alone.'

'Errol isn't the only male cat around Edgemarsh Lake,' I defended. 'I don't know why you should jump to the conclusion that he's to blame.'

Unfortunately Errol chose that moment to come ambling into the room, perhaps drawn by the sound of his own name, or perhaps curious to see what had distracted us from the vital business of getting his supper. He gave a chirrup of pleased surprise when he saw the feline in the stranger's arms and made straight for her, breaking into a raucous serenade. Pitti-Sing immediately began to struggle to get down and join him. It was abundantly clear that Errol was well known to her and had enjoyed the fullest cooperation in his escapade.

'No! No!' the man cried, clutching the squirming cat desperately. 'No, Pitti-Sing, stay with Daddy.' He glared at me. 'Get that monster out of here! Go away! Go away—' He launched out with one foot at Errol.

'No-o-o!' Tessa leaped to save Errol from the kick. As she bent to pick him up, the foot landed on her cast. 'Oooh!' she screamed and burst into tears.

'You kicked her! You kicked my sister!' Timothy was upon him like a whirlwind, fists flying.

'Oh my God!' The man dropped to his knees beside Tessa. 'I'm sorry, honey. I didn't mean to hurt you. It was an accident.' Pitti-Sing took advantage of his divided attention to twist free and break away. Errol followed her.

'Timothy!' I caught my son as he drew back his foot to aim a kick at the man's head, now within range, and pulled him away. 'Behave yourself! It was an accident. Tessa—' I knelt beside her—'are you all right? Let me see your arm, darling. Does it hurt to move it?' If that stupid man had rebroken her arm, I'd kick him myself.

'Mummy!' She hurled her good arm around my neck and subsided against me, still sobbing.

'My God, lady,' the man said. 'I'm sorry. I'm so sorry. I wouldn't have hurt her for the world. Honestly.'

'You were going to kick Errol,' Timothy accused. 'You wanted to hurt *him*.'

'Damn right!' For an instant, something dangerous sparked in the man's eyes. 'That cat has it coming to him!'

'He's an awful man, Mummy,' Tessa confided loudly. 'I don't like him.'

'I'm terrible,' the man agreed unexpectedly. 'Here—' He stuck out his chin and pointed it at Tessa. 'Go ahead and sock me. As hard as you can. Then we'll be even.'

'Tessa!' I caught her doubled-up fist. 'Two wrongs don't make a right! And you—' I turned to the man—'ought not to suggest such a thing. I'm trying to bring up my children to be civilized!'

'Sorry, lady, you're right.' He wrenched himself to his feet. 'I'm glad you stopped me. I'll bet that kid packs quite a punch.'

Tessa gave one final sniff and tried not to smile, 'I

could knock you over,' she said.

'Tessa!'

'Sure you could, kid.' He reached out as though to pat her on the head, but had second thoughts and withdrew his hand hastily.

'Look.' He turned to me. 'I'm sorry. I shouldn't have said what I said about your cat. I was angry. Believe it or not, I'm a reasonable man and you look like a reasonable woman, so why don't we compromise? I'll settle for having the cat taken care of.' So that I should have no doubt about his meaning, he added, 'I'll even pay the vet's bill myself.'

'No!' I said sharply. I couldn't possibly do that to someone else's cat. What would Nancy and Arnold say if they came back and found Errol neutered? Presumably they liked him the way he was or they would have attended to the operation themselves. Perhaps they had plans for breeding from him at some future time.

'So much for reasonable compromise.' A sulky look spread over the man's face.

'Mummy, he's still trying to hurt Errol, isn't he?' Tessa asked plaintively.

'It won't hurt the cat,' he snapped.

'It won't do him any good,' I countered, firmly on Errol's side. 'Why don't *you* be reasonable? They're both long-haired cats, the kittens ought to be beautiful.'

'I wanted to mate Pitti-Sing with one of her own breed when she was a bit older. She's a pure-bred Himalayan—' He broke off and looked around. 'Where is she? Where did she go? Pitti-Sing . . . here, Pitti-Sing . . .'

'He calls her Pitti-Sing,' Timothy observed with interest.

'It's not baby-talk' The man went on the defensive. 'It's from *The Mikado*. Pitti-Sing was the—'

'We're quite conversant with the works of Gilbert and Sullivan, thank you,' I said crisply.

'Say, that's right' He seemed struck by a new thought. 'You've all got accents. But—' He looked around and shook his head. 'This *is* the right house. I'm sure. Besides—' he said it like an accusation—'that cat was here.'

'The cat lives here,' I said. 'We don't. We've swapped houses with the Harpers for the summer. We're the Blakes. This isn't our house—or our cat.'

'That explains it!' His face cleared. 'No wonder you wouldn't agree about the cat. In that case, there's no problem. I'll take the thing to the vet myself. You don't have to know anything about it until it's all over. Then you can be as shocked and indignant as they are—and put all the blame on me.'

'No!' I was already shocked and indignant. 'Certainly not! That's unthinkable! Errol is under our protection— if you dare to lay one finger on him, I'll call the police!'

'Oh.' His sigh was a bit too theatrical; I mistrusted it instantly. 'I'm sorry you feel that way, but—' he sighed again—'I suppose there's nothing I can do about it. I'll just take my cat and leave. If that's all right with Errol—'

'Timothy, Tessa—go find the cats. Bring Pitti-Sing back here to Mr—?'

'I'm sorry,' he said. 'I'm Noah Peterson. My uncle has loaned me his house to work in for the summer. I guess that makes me your nearest neighbour. We ought to try to get on better.' He smiled and held out his hand.

'I suppose so.' Somewhat reluctantly, I shook it. In the sudden silence, I became aware of strange crackling noises in the background. 'What are those children doing now? Or is it the cats?'

'I don't know.' He frowned and listened. It was too far away to be the children. 'It sounds like a string of firecrackers going off. Some of the kids at camp must be staring their Fourth celebrations early.'

'Rather muted firecrackers—' I moved uneasily to the

window and raised the shade. A crimson light flickered in the sky. 'Perhaps they're sending up fireworks.'

'Oh no!' He strode over to the front door and opened it. 'Oh no!'

'What is it?' I followed him out on to the porch and the question became unnecessary. Now I could smell the smoke and hear the angry crackle of flames.'

'Tim! Tessa!' I called, fighting panic. It was the nightmare all over again, except that this time I was awake.

'Kids!' Noah Peterson said bitterly. 'They've set light to the bonfire. They're going to ruin the Fourth of July for everyone.'

'The bonfire . . .' I began to relax. 'At the top of the Lake . . .' It was a safe distance away. Furthermore, it would soon be under control. Already the swooping siren of a fire engine could be heard rushing along the road from town. 'That's all right, they'll soon have it out.'

'It will still be ruined,' he said gloomily. 'By the time they're through, it will never dry out again in time for Tuesday night.'

'Mummy—' Tessa came up behind us. 'I've got Pitti-Sing. Listen, she's purring.'

'Fine,' I said, although the sound could not be heard above the crackling noises.

'And I've got Erroll!' Timothy was flushed with triumph. Or perhaps it was just the reflection of the red glow overspreading the sky. 'What's that?'

'That's the Fourth of July gone up the spout!' Noah Peterson gathered his cat from Tessa's arms. 'Someone's set off the bonfire early.'

'Will there still be a Fourth of July?' Timothy asked uncertainly.

'Oh, sure. There'll still be the town picnic, the Horribles parade, the fireworks . . . but it won't be the same. Not without the Grand Finale Bonfire.'

'It still sounds like a full programme to me.' I tried to cheer him. He seemed to be a hidebound traditionalist—perhaps because of his interest in history.

'Oh well.' He tried to cast off his gloom. 'I suppose we might as well go down to the lake and watch it across the water. It's the only bonfire you'll see this year.' He started down the steps, then seemed to recall that he was still carrying Pitti-Sing. Timothy still clutched Errol.

'We'd better leave the cats in the house—if you don't mind,' he said. 'It might upset them.'

Pitti-Sing might be sensitive enough to be upset by the bonfire, but I doubted whether anything short of a charge of dynamite would ruffle Errol's fur. Nevertheless, I took Pitti-Sing from him and went into the house. Timothy followed me.

'Put them in separate rooms!' Noah Peterson called after us.

Everyone appeared to have had the same idea. The circumference of the lake was dotted by telltale points of light—pinpricks that were cigarettes, and larger circles that were flashlights. Voices carried on the still night air, with an occasional burst of laughter. The show might be going on ahead of schedule but everyone seemed determined to enjoy it just the same.

The noise was louder out here, a constant snapping crackling roar, punctuated by loud reports as a knot of wood exploded sending sparks showering upwards. The cracks were echoed from the camp across the water, where discipline had obviously slipped in the face of this unscheduled excitement and some of the campers were setting off their firecrackers early.

The air seemed even hotter and the smoke pall pressed down over the lake. I fought back an urge to cough and blinked my eyes against the acrid smoke.

'We're all right so long as the woods don't catch,' Noah

Peterson muttered to me.

'If there was any danger, why did they allow the bonfire to be built in the first place?'

'They've been building it up for weeks—the weather was all right when they started. Everybody for miles around drops by and adds their contributions to it—it's a matter of local pride to have the biggest and best bonfire in the state. Now it's all shot to hell!'

The first stream of water from the firemen's hoses hit the flames, producing a loud hiss and a cloud of steam. There were assorted boos and cheers from the watching crowd. Not everyone wanted to see the fun ended. Including, presumably, the one who had started the fire.

'Those kids—' Noah looked across the lake to the shore of Camp Mohigonquin. Suspicion must always fall on a group of slightly bored juveniles living away from home and under supervision that wasn't as strict as it might have been. 'They're going to have some explaining to do in the morning.'

'I don't know about that.' Unnoticed by me, another couple had strolled up to join us. 'The condition everything is in after this long dry spell, you can't rule out spontaneous combustion.'

'Hank, Viv—' Noah seemed to know them well. 'Let me introduce Mrs Uhh—' He broke off; he did not know me nearly so well.

'Rosemary Blake,' I said. 'And Tessa and Timothy.'

'Celia's sister.' Viv Singleton identified me immediately. 'We've been looking forward to meeting you. Celia's been talking about your visit for weeks.'

'Glad you finally made it.' Hank shook hands all round and nodded towards the fire. 'Just in time for all the excitement, eh?'

Another engine had joined the first two and all three were steadily pumping water on the flames. The fire was stubborn, just when it seemed contained, it burst out again at another corner of the ramshackle pile. The firemen would get it under control eventually, but it was going to take an awful lot of water. Noah's prediction that it would never dry out again in time for Tuesday night was obviously correct.

'Look at that son-of-a-bitch burn!' Hank gloated.

'Don't be such a schoolboy,' his wife scolded. 'Just because you're here to see it. Remember, it's going to spoil the fun for a lot of people. Most of them will be arriving tomorrow.'

'Summer people!' Hank abruptly remembered his companions. 'Sorry, folks,' he said to us. 'No offence meant.'

'None taken,' Noah assured him. 'We know you only hate your customers.'

'Hank can't stand parting with the best things,' Viv explained to me. 'I have to force him to sell. He'd be prefectly happy living like a packrat with everything towering over him.'

'We call it Early Collier Brothers decor,' Hank said. 'My ideal—so long as it's all antique.'

'If he starts on old newspapers, I throw him out,' Viv laughed.

'You must come and visit the shop,' Hank said. 'I've got some English pieces there I know you'll love.'

'I'd like to see it,' I said. 'But I'm afraid I'm not in the market for anything right now.'

'That's all right,' Viv said quickly. 'We also buy.'

'Nor have I anything to sell.' People seemed to expect me to be pretty free with the Harpers' possessions. 'Everything in house belongs to the Harpers.'

'Oh, we know that,' Hank said. 'What Viv is driving at is that we make regular buying trips to Europe. We'll be in England during the winter when business is quiet. If your taste is anything like your sister's, we'd be more than happy to take anything you're willing to part with.'

'Well, really—' It was a bit much. I'd just met them and they were practically making offers for my furniture. 'I'll have to think that over.'

'Sure you will,' Viv agreed. 'We didn't mean to pressure you. It's just that we don't want to miss a likely prospect. You come and see our shop. No strings attached—'

An earsplitting hoot ripped through the air, then another, and another.

'My God!' Noah said. 'That's the Fire Whistle! There's a fire in the town—and all the engines are out here at the lake!'

Confusion and consternation became apparent among the figures attending to the bonfire. One jet of water dropped and turned aside. The fire immediately leaped higher and the stream of water was directed back on the flames. Shouted consultations began.

'Send back the hook-and ladder,'' Noah groaned between clenched teeth. 'All the engines can pump water, but if the ladder is needed it will be needed fast and there won't be time to send for it if they leave it at the lake.'

The whistle stopped; the fire no longer seemed so noisy. I was just breathing a sigh of relief when the whistle began again, a series of short sharp blasts.

'. . . Five . . . six . . .' Hank was counting. 'Seven . . . eight . . . Eight blasts—that's the south side of town.'

'South! Oh, Hank—the shop!' Viv turned and ran towards the path to the road. Hank followed her.

The firemen seemed to have reached the same conclusion as Noah Peterson. The hook-and ladder began backing slowly while the firemen were still reeling in its hoses. Shouts of encouragement could be heard as they finished their task and leaped aboard. The engine rolled away from the fire and turned towards town. Someone switched on the siren and we could hear its swooping wail as the engine shot out of sight.

As the siren died away, there came another series of

small explosions. This time they signalled the slamming
of car doors as onlookers deserted the almost-tamed blaze
to go in search of the new excitement. Revving engines
sprang to life around the lake. Presumably some, like the
Singletons, would be going to check on their own interests
in town, but others would be mere sightseers.

The remaining firemen battled on stubbornly. It didn't
matter to them that they had lost half their audience;
they had to put out the fire and get back to town in case
they were needed.

'Mummy.' Timothy danced about restlessly, no longer
satisfied with the dying blaze at the far end of the lake.
'Mummy, can we go in to town and see the fire?
Please?'

'Better not,' I said. 'It's late and we've had a busy day.
It's way past your bedtime now.'

'It looks like a big one.' Noah Peterson was frowning
towards town where a fresh red glow was colouring the
sky. 'I'd better collect Pitti-Sing and shut her away, then
go and see if I can help. It will be all hands to the pump
with the other engines out at the lake.'

'I can help, too, Mum,' Timothy entreated.

'The less people underfoot, the better.' Noah Peterson
met my eyes. 'I don't like the looks of this,' he said grimly.
'Don't tell me it's starting here.'

CHAPTER 10

The nightmare came back that night. Mercifully I could
remember little of it as I woke. Only that, heart-
wrenchingly, John had been there again and, again, it
had been climaxed by that terrible hollow sound of the
coffin lid falling.

I struggled up on one elbow and stared into the

darkness. It was not yet dawn; the residual smell of smoke was everywhere.

It came from outside. Of course, it was outside. I could not quite make myself believe it. I got up and went on what was becoming my accustomed patrol.

The tiny night light glowed like a living spark at the electric socket at the end of the hall. Shaking off the disquieting thought, I looked into Timothy's room: it was dark, silent and peaceful. He was safe.

Tessa's room: dark, not quite silent. There was an uneasy rumbling somewhere in the darkness. I stepped inside the doorway. The rumbling intensified, two glowing sparks appeared at the foot of the bed. I choked back a cry and rushed forward. The sparks rose to meet me, the rumbling changed tone.

'*Prryah?*' a small voice inquired.

'Erroll!' I went limp with relief. 'You rotten beast!' I gathered him into my arms and tiptoed out of the room, closing the door behind us. 'I'm *sure* you're not allowed to sleep on the beds when your people are here. You ought to know better.'

'*Prryah,*' he said again and nuzzled my chin before lapsing into a low contented purr. He stayed in my arms while I completed my rounds, but slipped to the floor as we entered the kitchen and marched up to the refrigerator.

'*Mmmrreow!*' he said pointedly, staring at the door.

'Oh, all right.' I opened the door and dipped into a bowl of leftovers. 'Just don't expect to make a habit of this,' I warned him.

While he was gulping down his unexpected treat, I went round the ground-floor rooms. All quiet, all well. This lingering uneasiness must be the residue of the nightmare. I had already learned that the depression engendered by such dark half-remembered dreams could cloud the entire day. But it wasn't daylight yet. Perhaps if

I could manage to go back to sleep again, I could ward off the threatened gloom.

When I returned to the kitchen to snap off the light, Errol was licking his whiskers and sitting hopefully by the back door.

I opened the inner door obligingly, then hesitated with my hand on the latch of the screen door, suddenly overwhelmed by an indefinable sense of menace.

The air was heavy and sour with the thin acrid odour of wet ashes. A warm wind rustled dry leaves in a manner calculated to fan any incipient sparks. If a fire started out there in the woods, what chance would a small animal have?

'I don't think so, Errol.' I let my hand fall from the latch. 'I think we'd both better go back to bed.'

Errol seemed to agree. His fur bristled up on end and a low growl rose from his throat. He didn't like the look or the smell of it out there any better than I did. Then he gave a disdainful twitch of his whiskers and turned back into the kitchen, dismissing any idea of venturing outside.

'Quite right, Errol.' I shut the inner door and bolted it. 'Things will look better in the morning.'

The next time I awoke, it was to the sound of supressed giggles and the warm contented purring of Errol, curled in the curve of my shoulder and neck, his nose almost in my ear.

'Shhh—' Tessa's voice warned and I heard a rattle of crockery. 'Don't spill anything!'

I could keep my eyes closed no longer and opened them to find Timothy steadily advancing on me balancing a breakfast tray. 'Surprise!' he shouted, as he saw that I was awake.

'Darlings—how lovely! What a nice surprise!' I struggled to a sitting position, dislodging Errol. What was he doing there? I thought I had left him downstairs.

'I cooked it myself,' Tessa said proudly. 'Timothy just carried it up because I couldn't manage.'

'You did not!' Timothy placed the tray on my lap where it balanced perilously. 'I made the toast—and the tea.'

The toast was charred at the edges; tealeaves floated on top of the cup. 'It all looks delicious,' I assured them.

Errol agreed. He had been inspecting the tray with interest; breakfast in bed was something new in his experience, but he approved of it. With a pleased chirrup, he dived on the plate, snatching up a rasher of bacon and leaped off the bed with it.

'Stop him! Stop him!' Tessa shrieked. 'Rotten Errol! That wasn't for you. That was Mummy's!' She started after him with the obvious intention of reclaiming it for me.

'Let him go, Tessa. I wouldn't eat it now.'

Errol turned in the doorway, the limp bacon hanging down on either side of his mouth like a walrus moustache and gave one final crow of triumph. We heard him thudding down the stairs.

'Errol is a lot faster than Esmond,' Timothy said judiciously.

'And sneakier. We'll just have to be more careful with him around. We're not used to an undisciplined cat.'

'I wanted everything to be nice for you,' Tessa mourned, looking at the greasy trail across the sheet and the tea slopped into the saucer from Errol's dive across it.

'Never mind, I still have another rasher of bacon and this nice egg.' Secretly, I was not at all displeased. I have never liked breakfast in bed and this would discourage the children from such ill-considered acts of thoughtfulness.

The minor concert was playing outside for several minutes before it occurred to me that it might have anything to do with us. By the time I fought free of the mass of Sunday newspapers and got to the front door, Pixie Toller was standing on the porch about to ring the doorbell.

'There you are,' she said. 'I'd about given you up. Celia rang to say she isn't feeling well and asked if I could deliver the boys to camp today. Didn't she tell you?'

'No—what's wrong?' Luke was looking unconcerned in the front seat of the Welcome Wagon. Perhaps it wasn't serious.

'She thinks she may be coming down with a cold. Doesn't want to spread her germs around while she's in the infectious stage. Very public-spirited of her. I wish more people had that attitude.'

'Perhaps I ought to go over—'

'She'll be all right. If you ask me, it's just a sore throat from all that smoke last night. The bonfire was practically on their doorstep. It will take days for the house to air out.'

'Oh yes. And what—' I was reminded—'about that fire in town? The Singletons were afraid it might be their antique shop. Was it?'

'No, it was an empty building. An abandoned warehouse on the outskirts of town. It sure did burn—it was a two-alarm fire. They had to put in an emergency call for a couple of engines from the next town because of the two they had to leave out at the lake. We haven't had excitement like that for a long time.'

'Oh, I'm glad,' I said. 'Not that the building burned, I mean. I'm just glad it wasn't the Singletons' shop. They were so worried about it.'

'I should think they would be,' Pixie said. 'I'll bet they're not carrying half enough insurance. If you ask me, they're sailing a lot closer to the wind than is safe. Of course, that's true of a lot of people in this town. Only—'

her mouth twisted wryly—'some of us don't realize it until it's too late.'

Luke had grown restive; he left the car and bounded up the steps to join us. 'Isn't Tim ready?' he asked.

'I thought he wasn't starting at camp until tomorrow,' I said. 'Today is Sunday.'

'That's right—it's Registration Day. He can sign in with the new kids today and then stay on for the day. Nobody cares what happens today.'

'Well, go and find him then and explain.' I didn't care myself, I discovered. If that was the way things were arranged, we might as well fall into line.

'Why don't you and Tessa come along?' Pixie invited. 'We'll drop the boys at camp and then we can go in to town and view the ashes of the big blaze and have lunch.'

It sounded like a good idea.

There was a minor traffic jam on the road leading up to Camp Mohigonquin. A very high-class traffic jam. Cadillacs, Jaguars, Rolls-Royces and an astounding variety of custom-built foreign cars, some with chauffeurs at the wheel, were bumper-to-bumper along the road. Engines running, tempers visibly fraying, the occupants exchanged frosty smiles or looked straight ahead pretending the others weren't there at all.

'Oh—oh,' Pixie said. 'I always forget how grim it gets for the Changing of the Guard.'

'What?'

'That's what we call it hereabouts—with a due respect to you folks. It happens every two weeks. A few of the kids stay at the camp all summer, others are just there for two or four weeks. Their parents or—' her mouth twisted again—'the servants bring them and carry them away again. The camp opened for the summer two weeks ago, the first contingent is leaving today.'

'And the second contingent arriving.' Now that I knew

what to look for, I noticed small heads bobbing into sight behind the rolled-up windows of the air-conditioned luxury limousines.

'An awkward time for them to be arriving, isn't it? Right in the middle of a holiday weekend?'

'Bad timing,' Pixie agreed, 'but that's the way the calendar rolled round this year.' She threaded through a sudden opening in the traffic and both streams parted before her. She had the advantage of not having to worry about explaining dented fenders to an employer. 'I wouldn't be surprised if it was one of the kids who have to leave today who set off the bonfire. Didn't want to miss *everything*.'

It appeared that Pixie wasn't the only person in town to harbour that particular suspicion. The Chief of Police and two of his officers—one male and one female—were in heated debate with Greg and Lois.

'Hi, folks!' Dexter came over and lounged against the Welcome Wagon as Pixie stopped.

'Hi, Dexter,' Pixie said. 'How's your alibi? Looks like you guys are the number one suspects.'

'All this fuss over a bonfire—would you believe it?' Dexter rolled his eyes heavenwards. 'This would be a good day to rob a bank in town—all the fuzz is out here.'

'All of them?' I looked at the three intent individuals, who just barely outnumbered the camp authorities they were questioning. 'You mean that's all there is?'

'Except for a part-timer on the switchboard back at the station. How many do you want?' Pixie was indignant. 'Spare a thought for the poor taxpayers. These are enough—this is the first crime wave since Old Man Peterson went on a toot last Christmas and drove his old Ford through the windows of Gino's Place and wrecked the lobster tank.'

'Noah Peterson did that?' He was a very surprising man.

'Good heavens no! Not Noah. Old Jonah, his uncle. You won't meet him — unless you're here very late in the year — he disappears for the tourist season. Cantankerous old goat can't stand the summer people — not that he minds renting his place to them. It's amazing he's let Noah have it this year. I'll bet Noah's paying.'

'Maybe Old Jonah set off the bonfire to try to get us into trouble.' Dexter had his own theory. 'It's just the kind of thing he'd do. He hates Camp Mohigonquin.'

'Yes,' Pixie did not deny the charge. 'But he wouldn't bother to come down off his mountain just to get you in trouble. Unless —' She looked at Dexter sharply and then at Luke. 'Are you sure he *gave* you the old outhouse to put on top?'

'Uh, well . . .' Dexter squirmed uneasily. 'I guess maybe it was Old Noah who said we could have it. But he ought to know.'

'He'll know when Jonah comes back and finds it gone,' Pixie said. 'I wouldn't like to be in his shoes then.'

'Aw, it's only an old backhouse,' Dexter protested. 'He's got inside plumbing. Why should he get sentimental about a thing like that? Unless —' His eyes gleamed with sudden excitement. 'Maybe he hid his money in it. Maybe he had a cash box built into it somewhere. No burglars would ever think of looking there.'

'If he did, it's too late to think about it now.' Pixie winked at me. I was relieved to find she didn't believe it. It sounded all too plausible to me. The whole Peterson family was obviously quite eccentric.

'It's all gone up in smoke,' Pixie said with relish. 'If you think there's trouble now, just wait until Jonah gets back!'

'Aw —' Dexter's face cleared. 'I'll be gone by then.'

'I won't.' Luke looked worried. 'He'll be back when school starts. He's on the School Board.'

'Oh, Pixie, stop teasing them. There probably wasn't anything in it at all.'

'Well—' Luke would not be comforted. 'Old Man Peterson was awfully fond of it, I don't know why.' He brightened. 'Maybe it isn't all burned. Maybe we can get it down and put it back where it was.'

'Oh no,' Pixie said firmly. 'You'll do no such thing. You could kill yourself clambering over what's left of that junk heap. You're lucky you didn't hurt yourselves getting it up there in the first place.'

'My father helped before,' Luke said. 'He'd help us again.'

'I don't want you to have any part of this,' I told Timothy. 'One broken arm in the family is enough.'

The discussion with the police seemed to be breaking up in some acrimony. Looking hot and harassed, Greg came over to us while Lois led the police to the cookhouse.

'Trouble?' Pixie asked sympathetically.

'Nothing but.' Greg shook his head. 'They want all the kids placed under detention and then they want to interview them one at a time. I had to tell them that half the kids here right now are the new intake and the ones they really wanted to see left early this morning. They didn't like that.'

'I don't suppose they would.' Pixie clucked. 'Not that interviewing the kids would do them much good. None of these kids ever admit knowing anything.'

'And they may not,' Greg defended. 'They may all be perfectly innocent. The ones who are still here. Let's face it, if a camper set the fire, he'd have been one of the first ones away this morning. Chief Rogers knows it, too, that's why he's so mad. He should have been here at the crack of dawn to stop them before they got away.'

'All this fuss about setting off the bonfire early.' I was amazed.'They really don't have much of a crime problem in this town, do they?'

'It's not just the bonfire,' Greg said. 'The Chief thinks

the same person may have been responsible for the blaze in town. He isn't sure yet whether it was set deliberately or whether it was caused by sparks drifting down from the bonfire. Whichever way, he's blaming Camp Mohigonquin.'

'It isn't fair,' Dexter said. 'They always pick on us.'

'I wonder why?' Greg did not seem heartened by Dexter's championship.

'Come on, Luke, Tim—' Dexter opened the door of the Welcome Wagon impatiently. 'Let's get going. There's a lot of new kids in today—let's show them the ropes.'

'Just watch it, Dexter.' Greg's face was grim.

'Huh?' Dexter widened his eyes, looking improbably innocent. 'I don't know what you mean.'

'Oh yes you do. I mean—' Greg spelled it out—'no more Initiation Rites. We don't want a repeat of last year.'

'Aw, Greg, that was an accident.'

'You were damned lucky that kid's parents didn't decide to sue.'

'Aw, Greg . . .' Dexter had been backing away, now he turned and disappeared into a clump of pines. Luke and Timothy followed him.

'Will they be all right?' I looked after Timothy anxiously. 'What *did* happen last year?'

'Never mind,' Greg said. 'It's over and it will never happen again. I'll guarantee that. But it was a damned good thing for Dexter that he was here in camp last night and we can prove it.'

'It wasn't entirely Dexter's fault,' Pixie said. 'How was he to know the boy had a weak heart?'

'Not even his parents had suspected it,' Greg agreed, 'but it was a rough way to find out. And expensive—he was in an Intensive Care Unit for ten days. They were willing to be reasonable because no one had ever known about the weakness. The point is, it should never have happened.'

'It might be just as well it did,' Pixie argued. 'At least, when he goes to college, he'll know better than to let himself in for any hazing. Some Fraternities have actually killed a candidate or two in the past.'

'Listen,' Greg said. 'I'm not worrying about what might happen in the future. And I'm not worrying about what's happened in the past. I'm carrying the can for this gang here and now. From now on, we're going to run a tighter ship! Tonight I'll read them the Riot Act—and ban all campfires until we've had some rain. The episode is now closed!' He turned and strode away.

'Well!' Pixie murmured. 'Well, well, well!'

CHAPTER 11

Strange, the sadness a holiday can bring—even a borrowed holiday. The Fourth of July had nothing to do with us, except by ancient association—or, rather, dis-association—and yet an all pervasive heartache engulfed us. John was not here to see it.

As a family, we had planned an American holiday some day; we had talked about the delights of unfamiliar customs and celebrations of unknown festivities. Now, all the discussion, all the laughter, all the happy celebrations—all were dust and ashes.

The future had arrived and John was not here to share it with us.

Oh, we laughed at the eccentric costumes of the Horribles Parade, we drank the iced lemonade and ate the hot dogs, hamburgers and sandwiches at the Town Picnic, we applauded the fireworks display; but, before the first starburst had faded against the midnight blue sky, Tessa yawned and turned to me pleadingly.

'Can't we go . . . go back to the house now?' she asked. 'I'm tired.'

I knew that she had nearly said 'home' and then remembered where she was—and where her home was.

'Don't you want to see them try to light the bonfire?' Celia asked in surprise. 'They might be able to. They've pulled away the wettest wood and—' she laughed—'some of the kids have been out here with portable hair-driers trying to dry out the rest of it. There's a sporting chance it will catch. I hear they've been betting on it in the town.'

It would make another amusing little story to tell; another in-joke for the townspeople—another joke John would never share.

'I'm tired, too, Mummy.' Timothy leaned against me. 'Let's go now.'

The last time the sky had been bright with fireworks had been Guy Fawkes Night. John had been there last November, coaxing our bonfire to ignite. There were too many poignant memories being carried in the hot smoky night air.

'It's been a long day,' I apologized to Celia. 'Too much excitement. If the fire catches—' I added as a sop to her local pride—'we can watch it from the lakeshore, the way we did the other night.'

'All right,' Celia sighed. 'Just hold on a minute and I'll get Patrick to drive you home.'

'It seems a shame to drag him away from the festivities. Can't we just ring for a taxi? I don't want to be a nuisance to you.'

'Patrick will do it, don't worry. It may be quite a good idea. I think all the noise is getting on his nerves.'

Patrick did not seem to feel any sense of deprivation at being called upon to desert the festivities and drive us back to the house. He even joked a bit and only grew serious as we turned into Cranberry Lane.

'You know, you ought to apply for an International Drivers Licence, Rosemary,' he said. 'If you don't want to use the Harpers' car, you could pick up a cheap second-hand car while you're here and sell it again before you leave. It's not that anyone minds chauffeuring you around,' he added hastily. 'It's just that it would be better for you.'

'I know,' I said. 'I just . . . don't want to get behind a wheel . . . not yet.' I glanced into the back seat, but Tessa and Timothy were huddled together in the swift easy sleep of childhood. For a moment, I envied them. Then Tessa gave a soft whimpering cry and Timothy frowned and clenched his fists. Sleep was no longer such a desirable thing, after all. Perhaps they were beset by nightmares, too.

'Here we are.' Patrick slid the car to a silent halt. In the sudden stillness the night sounds grew louder: the frogs croaking by the lake; the trees stirring sporadically; the occasional hoot of an owl and, over all, the muffled explosions of the fireworks in the distance.

'Tessa, Tim—' I called softly. 'Come on, you can make it up to the house, can't you? You don't need Uncle Patrick to carry you. You're getting too big for that.'

'I'm too big for that,' Timothy echoed, lurching out of the car.

'So am I.' Tessa rubbed her eyes.

'Can you manage?' Patrick asked.

'Yes, thanks. Don't bother to get out.' I closed the doors quietly behind us. 'Celia and Luke will be waiting for you.'

'Well, if you're sure you're all right—' He gave us a smile, a wave of farewell, and the car moved off as quietly as it had arrived.

We walked up the path hand in hand watching the sky. The starbursts from the highest rockets could be seen above the treetops and showers of red, blue, green and silver illuminated the heavens before diving into the shadows of earth.

We were at the porch steps when an anquished yowl assaulted our ears.

'That's Errol!' Timothy snapped to attention, shaking off the last vestiges of sleep. 'Errol!' he called. 'Errol, where are you?'

The long answering yowl seemed to come from somewhere behind and above us.

'He's out here,' I said. 'Timothy, I told you to shut him in the house so that the fireworks wouldn't upset him.'

'I did,' Timothy protested. 'He must have got out when we weren't looking.'

'He's up a tree, from the sound of it.' We turned and moved in the direction of Errol's cries. 'I hope he can get down by himself, I don't fancy listening to *that* all night.

'If he can't, I'll go up and get him,' Timothy said. 'Or else we can call the Fire Brigade.'

'The Fire Brigade have more important things to do than—*ooof!*' I had collided with a dark solid shadow at the foot of the tree, too solid for a bush. 'What on earth—?'

'It's that man, Mummy,' Tessa said. 'What's he doing here?'

'A very good question, Tessa. Good evening, Mr Peterson, would you care to answer that question?'

'Good evening, folks.' Noah Peterson straightened up from his furtive crouch; he had obviously been hoping to escape notice. 'Did you have a good time at the fireworks? Or—' his voice expressed concern—'did something go wrong? You're home early.'

'What's he doing here, Mummy?' Tessa was not to be diverted.

'It's such a nice night—' Noah Peterson sounded as though he might be speaking between clenched teeth. 'I

just decided to take a little walk, that's all. I didn't mean
to trespass—'

'Why is Errol up that tree?' Timothy demanded. 'You
were trying to get him, weren't you? You were trying to
catch Errol and hurt him!'

Errol howled agreement and, now that reinforcements
had arrived, began a precarious backward skittering
descent of the tree-trunk.

'I wasn't going to hurt him,' Noah Peterson said. 'He'd
have had anæsthetic and excellent post-operative care.
I'd have taken him to the best vet in the State—the same
one who takes care of Pitti-Sing.'

'You admit it!' I was aghast. 'You were going to kidnap
the Harpers' cat and—and—'

'And have him neutered. It should have been done long
ago. They're anti-social to keep a brute in that condition.
He's a menace to every female cat in the neighbourhood.'

'That isn't for you to say!' Feeling rather catty myself, I
couldn't resist a dig. 'None of the female cats seem to
object. In fact, *yours* seems to have found him
particularly irresistible.'

Errol gave a final triumphant squawk and slid down
the last few feet of tree-trunk, fragments of bark spraying
out from his claws. He landed on the ground at our feet
and hurled himself at my ankles, purring wildly.

Noah Peterson stared down at Errol, his hands
twitching.

'You leave Errol alone!' Timothy swooped and caught
Errol up into his arms.'

'All right, Timothy, take Errol up to the house.' I
handed him the keys. 'You go, too, Tessa. I'll be along in
a minute. I just want to have a word with Mr Peterson.'

'Okay, okay.' Noah Peterson lifted his hands in
surrender. 'I apologize. Maybe I shouldn't have tried it.
But every time I look at Pitti-Sing, I get so damned
mad—'

'If you ever try it again, I shall call the police. Is that quite clear?'

'I'm sorry, I'm sorry.' He shook his head. 'I sure have got off on the wrong foot with you folks. Can't we start all over? Let's pretend we've never met before and—'

'It's been a long day,' I told him, 'and I'm too tired for games. I mean what I said. If you ever again—'

'You're tired,' he said, 'and I'm keeping you up. Good night.' He disappeared into the shadows.

I walked slowly up the path to the house. Noah Peterson might think I hadn't noticed it, but I had. At no point in our conversation had he given any undertaking not to try to get at Errol again.

After the long holiday weekend, the heat wave settled in with a vengeance. The thermometer hovered close to the 100°F mark and weather forecasters gave their reports with a grim relish: it was even worse in the South and Midwest; no relief was in sight anywhere in the Nation.

We lived on salad and iced drinks. It was easy to see why refrigerators and air-conditioners were necessities of life rather than luxuries. What amazed me was the way people refused to give way to the heat. Out of stamina, stubbornness, or the Yankee bloodlines that reached back to their *Mad-Dogs-and-Englishmen* heritage, everyone seemed to rush about, their only concession to the heat being the clothes—or lack of them—worn.

Timothy bronzed and thrived on it, but Tessa was nearly as wilted as I. We spent long sessions trying to puff talcum powder down inside her cast to relieve the discomfort. Other, longer, sessions were spent with Errol and tins of flea powder. It was impossible to keep him out of the woods and the woods were full of fleas, ticks and sand mites.

Pixie Toller seemed the most tireless person I had ever met. Her Welcome Wagon was never parked anywhere for very long. Of course, the summer people were arriving in their hordes and she was hard pressed to keep up with the stream of arrivals. I was grateful that she somehow managed to find time for us.

'I've got to do my store rounds—' Pixie had dropped in unexpectedly one morning. 'Come and help me. We'll collect the boxes of freebies, then you can come back to the house and we'll drink iced tea and pack another couple of dozen Welcome Baskets.'

'I'd love to,' I said. 'Tessa's up at Camp with Timothy today and I was just beginning to feel a bit bored—and blue.'

'I know.' Pixie nodded wisely. 'The first year is the hardest and yet everybody expects you to "snap out of it" and "pull yourself together" and all the other silly things. As though you'd lost your purse instead of your husband. They act as though it was a lamp that was broken—and not your whole life.'

'Oh! I hadn't realized you were a widow, too.'

'Grass, dear, not sod.' Pixie revved the engine and we leaped away from the kerb.

'I *beg* your pardon?'

'Oh, sorry. Over here we call a divorcee a grass widow. A sod widow is a woman who's buried her husband—he's lying underneath the sod, see? Mine—' her mouth twisted—'is lying somewhere else. And lying in every sense of the word, if I know him.'

'Oh, I'm sorry.' I decided not to go into any etymological explanations of my own. 'I hadn't realized . . . No one mentioned it.' And I would have a quiet word with Celia about that. Forewarned, I wouldn't have put my foot in it.

'Don't worry. It's such a common state nobody thinks anything about it at all. Only us walking wounded.'

I didn't say anything. I didn't really want to hear the story of Pixie Toller's life, but I had the uneasy realization that there was no way I could avoid it. We were driving along the main highway at forty-five miles an hour and I was literally a captive audience.

'Loss is loss,' Pixie said, 'and nobody knows what it feels like until it happens to them. That's the real gap between people, you know, not the Generation Gap. I divide people into two groups: the ones it hasn't happened to yet—and the rest of us. One way or another, it comes to us all eventually. The thing is, you're one of the lucky ones.'

'*Lucky?*'

'Sure. At least you know where your husband is! No, I'm sorry. I didn't mean that—not that way.' She reached over and patted my hand. The Welcome Wagon was doing forty-eight miles an hour now, as though trying to outdistance her thoughts.

'I mean,' she said, 'yours is a *clean* hurt. He didn't want to leave you. He died. He didn't come home one night and tell you he'd met somebody who really understood him. Younger, prettier—' The speedometer needle swung up to fifty, poised there momentarily, then went creeping upwards.

'And wasn't it lucky we hadn't had any children? We could have a nice neat break. No, there was no point in trying to talk it over. There was nothing left to say—' Her voice rose.

'Nothing left to say? I hadn't said anything at all. Of course, he was right. It was too late for talking. *She* was pregnant.'

Fifty-five . . . sixty . . . the highway sped past in a blur. I blinked my eyes and the road cleared. I hadn't realized I'd been so close to tears. It had been so different for me. John hadn't wanted to leave me and the children. *Where else would I be when you needed me?*

'Yes,' I said. 'You're right. John didn't leave of his own accord. He died in an automobile accident. It . . . it was a clean hurt.' I had never thought of it that way before.

'That's it,' she said. 'And I'm left with this dirty, miserable, festering hurt that will never go away and never be clean. Talk about automobile accidents—that's what frightens me sometimes. I have this recurring dream . . .'

Sixty-two . . . sixty-five . . . sixty-eight . . .

'I dream, too,' I said softly, but she didn't hear me.

'In this recurring dream . . . I'm driving the Welcome Wagon down a deserted road . . . and I see him ahead of me . . . walking along. He doesn't see me . . . his back is to me . . . he's walking away from me—again. He doesn't hear me . . . he doesn't know I'm there. I step on the gas . . .'

Seventy . . . seventy-two . . .

'Pixie—' We were approaching the outskirts of town. The speed limit signs read: thirty m.p.h.

'He turns . . . he sees me . . . for a minute, he's afraid . . . then he smiles . . . he waves . . . he thinks he can make a fool of me again. I know . . . he's going to make up . . . to come back to me . . . to take up where we left off . . .'

Seventy-five . . . seventy-seven . . .

I reached over stealthily, switched off the ignition and removed the key.

'And I hit him!' Pixie's knuckles were white from her grip on the steering-wheel. She hadn't even noticed what I'd done.

'He sort of goes *splat!* all over the radiator . . . and I can see his hands clutching at the radiator cap . . . then sliding, sliding away . . . as he goes under the front wheels . . .'

Seventy-seven . . . seventy-five . . . seventy-three . . .

Pixie was grinding her foot on the accelerator in her agitation. If I hadn't removed the key, we'd be doing over one hundred now.

'He keeps calling out to me . . . *"Come back"* . . .
"Come back." So I go back. I back up right over him . . .
then I go forward over him again . . . and back again . . .
I can feel the bump every time the wheels go over his
body . . . and I do it again and again . . .'

Sixty . . . fifty-five . . . fifty . . . I began to breathe more
easily.

'And when I finally stop and go back to look at him . . .
he's spread out like a mat—and he has WELCOME printed
right across his back. And I keep on saying, "I'll
'Welcome' you! I'll 'Welcome' you!' . . . and—' She looked
across at me in bewilderment, coming back to the
present.

'And that's where I wake up.' The Welcome Wagon
coasted to a stop and Pixie burst into tears.

I found that my hands were shaking. I waited for her to
regain control.

'Look, Pixie,' I said, as the emotional storm abated,
'why don't we call it a day? I mean, you can go to the
shops tomorrow just as well. Why don't we—?'

'No!' Pixie dabbed at her eyes savagely. 'I'm all right
now. Sorry. I haven't let my hair down like that since I
can't remember when. But it's all over now. Business as
usual—' She reached out automatically for the ignition
key and looked at the empty keyhole in surprise.

'I'm sorry—' I held the key out to her. 'I'm afraid I took
it. We were going so fast—and the town was straight
ahead. I got frightened—'

'Probably just as well.' Pixie took the key and stabbed
at the keyhole several times before fitting it in. Her
emotional upset wasn't as over as she'd have me believe.

'Pixie—' I tried again. 'I really do feel it would be
better if you didn't try to do anything more today. Let's
go back to the house and I'll make a salad for lunch and
you can rest in the hammock this afternoon.'

'No!' Pixie was on the verge of shouting. 'No, I can't!

I've already telephoned the stores—they'll have everything ready for me to pick up. Can't you understand? I *need* this job! I don't know—I don't know *what* I'd do without it!' She burst into tears again.

'All right.' I got out and walked round to the driver's side. 'Move over, Pixie. I . . . I'll drive.'

CHAPTER 12

'*You should have seen her, darling,*' I told him. '*She quite frightened me. Who could have imagined it? That nice, friendly, outgoing woman, so extrovert and funny—and that smouldering volcano of violence underneath.*'

'*Poor Pixie,*' John said. '*It sounds as though she's been through a terrible experience and had no one to blow off steam to—until you came along. She knew you'd understand.*'

'*You understand, too.*' That was why I loved him—one of the reasons. He always understood.

'*Perhaps, but you have the experience fully to understand. You know—*'

'*No,*' I denied. '*Please, no.*' He was trying again to guide me to some knowledge I did not wish to possess. I fought against knowing. It was pleasant here; we were happy. Why did he have to bring up that?

We were sitting in some odd but reassuring No-Man's-Land that seemed to be partly our living-room at home and partly the Harper kitchen in New Hampshire. It puzzled me slightly but I had stopped wondering why. We were together, that was all that was important.

'*All right, Rosemary.*' He smiled at me sweetly and sadly. '*All right—for just a little longer.*'

As usual, we were discussing the day's events over a

nightcap before going up to bed. We always saved up the amusing incidents and stories to tell each other at the end of the day. It occurred to me that I was doing all the talking, but I didn't want to follow through on that train of thought. I rushed on, speaking too quickly, too intensely, trying to hold the treacherous knowledge at bay.

'*It was awful. And dangerous. She was driving so fast —*' No — I didn't want to think about that, either.

'*I mean, Poor Pixie, to think of her having such awful dreams . . .*' My voice faltered. '*Dreams . . .*'

'*Steady, Rosemary, you're doing fine.*'

'*I don't want to do fine! Not without you! But it's all right, you're not like Pixie's husband, are you? You'll never leave me, will you? You'll never leave us?*'

'*Part of me will always be with you, Rosemary. With you and Tessa and Timothy —*'

'*Part isn't good enough! Promise me! Promise me!*'

'*Shh, Rosemary, shh . . .*' His face was sad, so sad, and I knew that it was not that he would not promise me, but that he could not. I was trying to fight a battle I had already lost.

'*Then take me with you. I don't want to be here without you —*'

'*There are the children to think of, Rosemary.*' He was holding me lightly in his arms. '*Tessa and Timothy need you.*'

'*Yes, the children. That was why I was so frightened when Pixie began driving so fast —*' Pixie and her problems seemed a safe subject to get back to. '*She was way over the speed limit. I was afraid she'd lost control and go off . . .*' my voice faltered, '*off the road . . .*' This was not such a safe subject, after all.

'*Or crash into something —*' I rushed on, unable to stop myself.

'*I was afraid we'd crash . . . and Tessa and Timothy*

would be orphans—' My voice broke. '*Orphans . . .*'

A deep imperative sound ripped through the gossamer world and I felt myself falling into consciousness. The sound came again and again, forcing recognition. I sat up and found myself counting automatically.

'Mummy! Mummy!' Timothy rushed into the room. 'It's another fire!'

'Mummy—' Tessa's voice was unsteady. 'It isn't anywhere near us, is it?'

'I don't know.' I snapped on the bedside lamp. Both children were wide awake and unlikely to go back to sleep easily.

'I'll find out.' Timothy darted for the doorway.

'Timothy! Where are you going?'

'Downstairs. They've got the code in the front of the telephone book. You keep counting—'

The whistle stopped, then started again, long insistent blasts, neatly grouped so that everyone could count them and identify the location of the blaze.

'Six blasts.' Timothy returned, bearing the telephone directory importantly. 'That's to the east of town. There isn't much out there except farmland. It's probably just an old barn.' He sounded disappointed.

'I hope it's nothing worse.' I looked at my watch: four a.m. At home, at this time of the year, dawn would be well advanced; here, the sky was still dark.

'When I grow up, maybe I'll be a fireman,' Timothy said thoughtfully. 'But it isn't as exciting at home as it is here. We don't have whistles so that everybody can know where the fire is. Why don't we, Mummy?'

'Not every place has it here.' Celia had explained the system to me. 'It's left over from the old days in smaller cities and towns. Before they had Fire Departments, most of the people in town were in the volunteer Bucket Brigade. The whistle was their signal to turn out and rush to fight the fire. They had to know where to go, so they decided on the code. It was rudimentary, but effective. People still use it because they still want to know where any fires are.'

'I don't like it.' Tessa was white-faced and fretful. 'It woke me up.'

'It was supposed to, silly.' Timothy was scornful. 'What would be the good of a fire alarm that didn't wake anyone up? It was supposed to get people out to fight the fire.'

'Let's go downstairs and get a cool drink.' I offered distraction. 'Then perhaps we can get back to sleep again.'

The wail of sirens in the distance carried on the still, heavy air; the smell of smoke already seemed to be encroaching. I hoped it *was* only a barn on fire.

In the morning, smoke still seemed to hang heavy in the air. Had the woods caught alight? I turned on the television for the newscast.

Now that we had discovered it, our set was permanently tuned to Channel 9—WMUR-TV—the Public Service Broadcasting station in Manchester, New Hampshire. They carried better programmes than most commercial channels and their coverage of local news was excellent.

'. . . serious fire in the Edgemarsh Lake District—' The screen sprang into life. The camera cut from the commentator's concerned face to a scene of charred and smoking ruins, while the voice-over continued:

'A piece of local history has been lost for ever with the destruction of the Old Tithe Barn early this morning. Firemen fought valiantly to save the building but the blaze was already too far advanced by the time the fire was discovered. More seriously, it is feared that a life, or lives, may have been lost in the fire—'

The camera cut to the twisted metal frames of two

backpacks. 'It is feared that hikers may have taken shelter in the barn for the night. Firemen are sifting the ashes now . . .'

Tessa whimpered and I snapped off the television.

'Don't worry, Tessa,' Timothy said. 'Maybe they got out safely.'

'Without their backpacks?'

'Yes, if they didn't have much time.' It was a chance to bring home a lesson without seeming to preach. 'It was more important to save themselves than anything they might be carrying. Lives are more important than possessions.'

Timothy nodded wisely, Tessa looked thoughtful. I glanced through the window at the woods outside. They no longer seemed charming and picturesque—only dangerously close to the house.

The day was off to a bad start and didn't improve as it wore on. The post brought a letter from Nancy Harper detailing several points about Cranberry Lane house-keeping she had forgotten to leave notes about; she made up for it by explaining exhaustively. As a *PS*, she added:

> I wonder if you're finding my old friends and neighbors as strange as I'm finding yours? Was Lania always so bloody-minded (you see how I'm picking up the lingo!) about that silly hedge? Arnold didn't mean to run into it—he just isn't used to a manual clutch. Besides, it will grow out better than ever next year for having a good pruning back now. Fortunately, the kids are getting along like a house afire.
> PPS: Esmond is fine and dandy and sends you his love. Give Errol a great big kiss for me.
> > Nancy.

I put down the letter and met Errol's knowing look. 'Consider yourself kissed,' I said. 'That's as far as I'm prepared to go.'

Errol blinked at me, then got up and strolled away.

'All right, be like that,' I called after him. He gave a final twitch of his tail and disappeared under a bush.

I turned back and realized that it was not I who had offended him. Noah Peterson was walking up the path, a tentative smile on his face. No wonder Errol had left.

We had not seen Noah Peterson during the fortnight since we had caught him trying to catnap Errol and I had hoped that we would have no further encounters with him.

'Good afternoon, Mrs Blake.' It seemed that he had worn an antiquated straw boater, possibly his uncle's, simply to be able to doff it in a suitably humble manner.

'Allow me to introduce myself,' he said quickly before I could speak. 'My name is Noah Peterson. I am ordinarily a respectable law-abiding citizen. I pay my taxes, keep up my alimony payments, go to church—perhaps not as often as I should—help old ladies across the street and desire only to live in peace with my fellow men—and women. I'm your nearest neighbour up here and I think we ought to get to know each other.

'So I've come over to invite you and your charming children to have dinner with me tonight at Gino's place. Or tomorrow night, if you already have plans for tonight. Or the night after that. Any time you say, but please, Mrs Blake, let's try to be friends.'

'Well . . .' It was a disarming speech—and obviously intended to be. I wondered how long he had rehearsed it. I also wondered whether I could trust him. If he got us all out of the way some night, would he arrange for someone to swoop on poor Errol and carry him away for the dastardly deed to be done while we were dining with him and providing his alibi?

'Please, Mrs Blake. I know we got off on the wrong foot. Can't we just forget about that and pretend that this is our first meeting—the way it should have been? Let's start all over again, hmmm?'

'Well . . .' It was perfectly true, we ought to be friends with our nearest neighbour. (Fleetingly, I wondered if Lania would still be speaking to me when we got home. It sounded as though Arnold had done quite a job on her precious hedge.)

'Please?' He gave me his warmest smile.

'All right.' I came to a decision. 'How do you do, Mr Peterson. How nice of you to come round and introduce yourself. I'm very pleased to meet you and, thank you, we'll be happy to have dinner with you.'

'Tonight?'

'All right.' Why not? 'Tonight.'

'Great! Marvellous!' He caught up my hand and wrung it. 'I can't tell you how happy this has made me. This is the way it should be. And—' he nodded conspiratorially—'we'll never even think about those other meetings again.'

Perhaps he wouldn't, but the children weren't going to forget it in a hurry. We would have to have a little heart-to-heart about letting bygones be bygones before they sat down at a table with Noah Peterson. We would also leave Errol safely locked up in the house.

I smiled enigmatically.

'I'll make the reservations at Gino's Place for tonight,' he said. 'And I'll come by and pick you folks up at about seven.'

Gino's Place was crowded when we got there. Gino greeted us like old friends and led us to a corner table at the back. A large lobster tank was in the centre of the room—presumably relocated since Norah's uncle had demolished the original one in the window. Large sinister dark blue-green crustaceans lurched across the bottom of the tank in unsteady progress, occasionally colliding with and crawling over each other. I saw that small pegs had been inserted into the joints of their claws so that they could not fight.

'Would you like lobster?' Noah asked. 'You can choose your own from the tank and they cook it while you wait. That way, it's really fresh.'

'No, thank you.' I shuddered. 'I'd feel like a murderer.' The children, looking rather ill, nodded agreement. 'Let's have something that I don't have to sentence to death.'

'As you wish. The menus will be along in a minute.'

Other people had no such qualms. We watched as a smartly-dressed couple debated briskly at the tank while their waiter stood by. It appeared that Gino's cousin Rudi had got his promotion to the main dining-room. When they indicated their choices, Rudi rolled up one sleeve, plunged his arm into the tank and caught up the luckless lobster which he transferred to his other hand before plunging back into the tank for the second lobster. It tried to escape, scrabbling frantically across the tank and trying to hide behind a conch shell. Uselessly. Rudi dragged him dripping from the tank and bore both lobsters—claws waving wildly—to the kitchen. The other diners applauded.

'Don't worry,' Noah told an appalled Tessa, who was on the verge of tears. 'They say the lobsters don't feel a thing. They plunge them straight into a vat of boiling water and . . . er . . . it's over instantaneously.'

'*Who* says they don't feel a thing?' Timothy demanded. 'Do the lobsters say it? They're the only ones who'd really know.'

'Well, never mind,' Noah said comfortingly. 'We've already decided we're not going to have lobster. Now—' he rustled his menu—'let's decide what we are going to have.'

Perhaps Americans have become desensitized to

violence. Their television sets pour out a constant stream
of muggings, murders, car crashes, beatings, rapes and
other horrors masquerading as entertainment. There
were nights when the News was even worse. Even driving
along their highways, one had to constantly avert one's
eyes from the squashed bodies of small animals who had
tried to cross the road against the stream of endless
traffic. So much violence everywhere. Perhaps they didn't
even notice it any more.

'I'll have the baked scallops,' Noah ordered. He leaned
forward and confided. 'Pitti-Sing is exceptionally fond of
scallops. I'll ask for a doggie-bag, in this case a kitty-bag,
at the end of the meal and bring some home for her.'

'I'll have the broiled liver,' Timothy said. 'And I'll have
a kitty-bag, too. Errol is crazy about liver.'

'I'll have a kitty-bag—' Tessa went straight to the
point. 'And then I'll have fried chicken. Chicken is Errol's
absolutely favourite food.'

'And you, Rosemary?' Noah was looking disgruntled. It
had not been his intention to provide a banquet for the
animal he hated with a deadly passion. 'What, in your
opinion, is the food Dear Errol most likes to eat?'

'Errol,' I said flatly, 'will eat anything that doesn't eat
him first.' I continued to study the menu. I seemed to
have lost my appetite since the episode of the lobsters.

'May I suggest the Steak Diane, madame?' Rudi leaned
over me solicitously. 'It is cooked at the table before your
eyes—very delicious.'

'Not tonight.' It was irrational to dislike the man
because he had done his job, but I couldn't help it. I tried
to keep the distaste out of my voice. 'I think I'll have the
Chef's Salad.'

'Very good, madame.' Rudi deftly twitched the menus
out of our hands and disappeared. The wine waiter took
his place and went into a huddle with Noah over the
Wine List.

'Look, Mummy,' Timothy said. 'Look who's over there. It's Greg and Lois!'

They looked up, alerted as he called out their names. For a fleeting instant there was a curiously hunted look on both faces.

'Hi, Greg! Hi, Lois!' Timothy waved to them. 'Who's minding the camp?'

'Timothy!' He was learning bad manners from his new friends.

Greg and Lois exchanged glances, then rose reluctantly and came over to our table. I began to understand the hunted look: a Camp Counsellor is never off duty. Not when there's a parent or child anywhere in the vicinity.

'Hello, Mrs Blake,' Greg said resignedly. 'Hi, Tess, Tim, Noah . . .'

Lois echoed his greeting. She was wearing a cool dark green full-skirted frock tonight, the lighter green jade frog swung from a gilt chain around her neck. I was suddenly glad that frog's legs weren't on the menu.

'Benjie Adams is holding the fort tonight.' Greg answered Timothy's question, looking directly at me. He evidently thought I might be worried about who was minding the camp. 'He's Deputy Administrator. You haven't met him yet because he's just arrived. He took a little vacation after his college term ended. Very good man—all the kids like him.'

'I'm sure they do,' I murmured, since he seemed to be expecting some response.

'Benjie worked for us last year, too. Maybe you remember, Noah? He's terrific at woodcraft, swimming and archery—'

'Hey, Greg, climb down, boy,' Noah said soothingly. 'You don't have to sell us. What's the matter? Chief Rogers on your back again?'

'And how!' Greg passed a weary hand across his forehead. 'They're trying to pin the new fire on the

Camp. He was up there all morning—and it was the Changing of the Guard again. He's working on the theory that's got something to do with it. He's got this crazy idea that arson has become some sort of passing-out ceremony.'

'It's mad!' Lois said heatedly. 'Totally mad! None of the kids would do a thing like that. Besides, I did the bed-check myself last night. They were all in their beds and sound asleep long before the fire started. And when those kids sleep, it would take an earthquake to wake them. I tried to tell Chief Rogers that, but he wouldn't believe me. He thought I was lying to protect my job.'

'You can see how he'd figure that way.' Greg was trying to be fair. 'Maybe we *would* lie if our jobs were at stake—but they aren't. He can huff and he can puff all he likes, but there's no way he can close down the Camp just because he's suspicious of it. We're booked almost solid right through to Labor Day and he hasn't the authority to close us down—' Greg's voice was rising. 'We'll take it to Court and put up such a fight that it will be *his* job on the line!'

'Greg—' Lois plucked at his sleeve. 'Greg, take it easy.'

'I can see you had quite a session with Chief Rogers,' Noah said drily.

'It isn't funny.' Abruptly, Lois turned hostile. 'That was a terrible fire—people died! Chief Rogers has no right to even suggest any of our campers had anything to do with it. We could sue him for libel!'

'Slander,' Noah corrected automatically. 'Libel is written, slander is spoken.' They didn't appreciate it.

'Let's get back to our table, Greg,' Lois said coldly.

'Sure' Greg started to turn away—which gave him a clear view of the entrance. 'Oh-oh,' he said, 'look who's here.'

Dexter came through the doorway and was half way towards a table for two marked RESERVED when he seemed to become conscious of watching eyes. His anticipatory smile faded, he sighed and came over to us.

'Hi, everybody,' he said. 'Hi, Greg.'

'Hello, Dexter,' Greg said. 'What a surprise seeing you here. I don't recall giving you a Late Pass.'

'Uh, no, you didn't. Benjie did. Aunt Luci turned up unexpectedly and wanted me to have dinner with her. She's touring the Straw Hat Circuit on a pre-Broadway tryout and they're starting in Manchester next week.'

'Is that a fact?' Greg sounded unbelieving. A collective gasp from the diners made him look over at the doorway.

Lucienne Tremaine made an entrance, came over to join Dexter, allowed us to be introduced to her and bore Dexter off to the reserved table.

'I guess,' Greg said, 'Benjie *did* give Dexter a Late Pass. I would have, too.' They went glumly back to their table.

'What was that all about?' I asked Noah. 'Is Lucienne Tremaine really Dexter's aunt, or is it a courtesy title?' It would have been hard to believe, except that Lucienne Tremaine *was* sitting at a table for two with Dexter, smiling as he ordered from the menu. Our waiter was bowing almost double every time she uttered a word. It was clear that he thought this was more like it.

The rest of the diners had resumed their conversations, although still casting envious glances at our table—and at Dexter. It was obvious that most of the male diners thought Dexter didn't deserve such luck.

'I believe she's an extended-family aunt of some sort. Through one of his mother's marriages—or perhaps one of his father's. Do you mean to say—' Noah looked at me curiously—'you don't know who Dexter *is?* Doesn't the name Dexter Herbert ring any bells at all?'

'He's Dexter Herbert *the Fifth*,' Timothy prompted. 'And he's going to give us free tickets to his father's new film.'

'Good heavens!' It all fell into place. 'Is *that* who he is? I never heard his surname before, he was just introduced to me as Dexter. He really is—is—' I remembered *the Fifth*—'in direct line of succession?'

'One of our great stage families,' Noah said. 'They may not be the Barrymores, but they've run them a pretty close second across the years.'

'I never expected to meet anyone from that family,' I said. 'What on earth is he doing at Camp Mohigonquin?'

'Going through the awkward stage. His mother doesn't want him around to remind her Public that she has a son that old; and his father doesn't want him around until he's lost seventy-five pounds, preferably more. So Dexter has been star boarder all summer long at Camp Mohigonquin for the past two years. In the winter, they send him to boarding-school.'

Rudi brought our orders and set them in front of us with the air of one throwing pearls before swine. He disappeared into the kitchen again. When he returned, he was wheeling a laden trolley on which a small conflagration blazed merrily. He careered through the dining-room with it, coming to a dramatic stop at the Tremaine-Herbert table.

'Hasn't he got that spirit lamp turned rather high?' I asked uneasily.

'He likes it that way,' Noah said. 'Makes a bigger effect. Just watch. Lucienne Tremaine is about to learn that she isn't the only one who can give a performance.'

Indeed, most of the room was watching. All that was lacking was a spotlight. With a flourish, Rudi dropped a dollop of butter into the shallow frying-pan and added the steaks when it began to sizzle. Apparently, both Dexter and his aunt had ordered the Steak Diane. No wonder Rudi was not going to waste his time on lesser appetites.

He turned the steaks, then poured brandy into a larger sized copper ladle than I would have used and set it

alight. With loving care, he poured the blazing spirit over
the steaks. Yellow flames billowed upwards, then
changed to blue. The blue flames raced round and round
the frying-pan, flickering, then spurting upwards with
fresh fury, persistent, unwilling to die out. When they did
begin to show signs of exhaustion, Rudi carefully tipped
in a ladle of vermouth which set the whole thing off
again.

Bemused, we all stared at the small inferno. I was quite
happy that I had not ordered the Steak Diane—what
would be left of the steak after all this was not something I
cared to contemplate. Others obviously felt differently; I
was aware of audible sighs of envy from surrounding
tables.

Gino himself brought their meals to Greg and Lois.
Absently I looked over—and was startled by the
expression on Lois's face. Why should she suddenly look
so horrified? I followed her gaze.

She, too, was staring at the blazing frying-pan and I
was abruptly in tune with her thoughts: the fires. Slowly,
fearfully, her gaze crept round the tables.

Lois was a Registered Nurse; her training would have
included a course in abnormal psychology. Could she
identify the arsonist in our midst? Or did she only think
she might? Her suddenly cool professional gaze halted at a
certain face.

Oh no—not Dexter! And yet, it was the classic
retribution of a rejected adolescent. Dexter was staring
avidly at the flames, a strange expression on his face.
That didn't mean he was a firebug. But the rapt
fascination with which he stared into the flames was
disturbing. Certainly, he was clever enough to time the
fires so that the outgoing campers would seem guilty if
suspicion fell on the camp.

I looked away, disliking myself for even entertaining
the thought—although it was Lois who had unwittingly

planted it in my mind. I glanced at her again.

Now she was looking directly at Greg. He was staring at the flames with a dark brooding expression that revealed a different side to his character. He was no longer Good Old Greg—everybody's pal. Greg the Ghoul was more like it. He was suddenly transformed into someone I would not like to meet alone on a moonless night.

Lois seemed to feel that way, too. She was frowning with concern and leaned forward as though to speak to him and break the spell, then seemed to think better of it.

Still the flames danced on. With another flourish, Rudi selected a tin from the rack, aimed the nozzle at the frying-pan and sprayed something over it. The flames flickered and died.

There was a burst of applause from the audience. The lights returned to their normal brightness—I had not realized that they had been dimmed—and all the dark shadows disappeared. People were themselves again.

'Some production, eh?' Noah and the children had joined in the applause. I had not.

'Yes,' I said. Lois still looked frightened and worried. I could not blame her. 'Quite . . . spectacular.'

CHAPTER 13

I rang Celia in the morning to suggest we carry out that long-projected shopping expedition into Boston. All of us. Especially the children. The bright sunshine had not quite dispersed the shadows of the night and I had begun planning ways to wean them away from Camp Mohigonquin—just in case. I no longer felt that they were in such good hands there.

'We might as well,' I urged. Celia was curiously reluctant. 'I've given up hoping for cooler weather.

Anyway, the stores are all air-conditioned. We'll be more comfortable inside than out. Unless you feel the drive is too much for you?'

'Oh no.' Celia had always hated admitting to weakness. 'It's just that—' She broke off and I could almost hear her mental calculations.

'You may be right,' she said. 'Patrick won't want to come—cities and crowds make him too nervous these days—but I'll bring Luke. There'll be Sales on and it isn't too early to be think about back to school clothes. The only thing is, I'll have to stop and do an errand on the way.'

'That will be fine,' I said. 'We're in no hurry.'

The postman brought another letter from Nancy—and I hadn't answered her first one yet. I was oddly disinclined to open it. It was not that reading about what was going on at home would bring too many memories flooding back—they had never left me.

Perhaps it was that I simply did not want to be faced with any more proof that my life—all the important parts of it—was out of my control. Now another woman and her family occupied my home and, inevitably, there must be changes. (How much of the hedge was destroyed? Would Lania blame me for allowing strangers to disrupt our quiet little world?) I looked at the smooth curving American writing on the envelope and knew that I did not wish to read any more unsettling bulletins.

Then I reminded myself that Nancy was Patrick's cousin. He was bound to inquire after her. Perhaps she had written to him, too, and he would question me about information we were both presumed to share. With some trepidation, I slid my finger under the flap and ripped open the envelope.

'Dear Rosemary—' Nancy wrote with more formality

than was usual with her. 'I haven't heard from you yet
and I hope everything is all right.'

I began to feel somewhat less beleaguered. Nancy, too,
must be having her own doubts about turning her home
over to strangers.

Don't be afraid to tell me if it isn't—I know how these
things can happen. If Errol has thrown up on the
living-room carpet again, don't worry about it. That
carpet has spent more time in the cleaners than it has
on the floor. We have a charge account there, so just
call them up and tell them to come over and collect it.

Errol strolled into the room just then and I looked at
him with new surmise. 'How's the old tum?' I asked
suspiciously. 'Feeling all right? If it isn't, you can get right
out of here—I have enough to contend with.'
Errol twitched his whiskers huffily, sharpened his claws
on a corner of the sofa just to show me whose territory this
was, then turned and made a dignified exit. I went back
to Nancy's letter.

I hope I don't sound paranoiac or anything—but I
haven't heard from a living soul over there since
I left. I'm beginning to feel as though some great
catastrophe the Powers That Be are keeping from us
has wiped the whole continent off the face of the
earth and everybody is afraid to admit it. When you
see Patrick, tell him he's a lousy fink for not writing.

I found myself smiling and reading the letter became
less of a chore. Nancy was sharp and funny, her pen-
pictures of my old friends, and neighbours were
recognizable, although oddly askew, viewed through her
New England eyes. I wondered if she would think the
same if I wrote her my impressions of Pixie Toller, Greg,
Lois, Noah Peterson and the rest. I must get down to a
letter to her—perhaps tomorrow.

I had relaxed too soon. Nancy's PS carried a sting in the tail:

By the way, I'm awfully sorry about this—but you know that Victorian jardiniere in the hall? Well, the kids were trying their new roller-skates—it had to be inside, because it was raining as usual—and Donald crashed into it. It's good and sturdy. When I picked it up, there were just a few chips missing (I'm afraid Donna crushed them to powder under her skates before she could stop herself.) But I rubbed over the chipped places with my green eyeshadow—it was almost a perfect match—and, really, you'd never notice it was damaged. Of course we'll buy you a new one—I mean, a replacement. I do hope you'll forgive us. It was an accident and couldn't be helped.

For a start, she could have kept her little monsters from making a skating rink out of my front hall—

'Mummy—' Tessa had been watching outside. 'Auntie Celia's here.'

'Fine, darling.' I pulled myself together and determined to stop worrying about what couldn't be helped. 'Call Timothy and we'll be off.'

Patrick was in the front seat, along with Luke. Celia was driving. 'You lot get in back,' she said. 'Patrick is just hitching a lift to town with us. We'll leave him off and then we won't be so crowded.'

'I have a message for you, Patrick,' I said, getting in. 'Someone thinks you're a lousy fink.'

'You've heard from Nancy!' He turned round, eyes alight with pleasure. 'How is she? What does she think of things over there? What else did she say?'

Celia ground the gears as we leaped away from the kerb.

'Here, read it for yourself—' I handed the letter to him. He took it eagerly. 'She wants a letter from you.'

'She hadn't sent me one.' His voice was aggrieved.
'Unless—' he brightened—'it's in the post. Maybe she's
had a letter-writing session and sent off a lot at once.
Look, Celia—' he waved the missive at her. 'A letter from
Nancy! Isn't that great?'

'Yessss,' Celia hissed.

'Do you mind—' Patrick turned back to me—'if I hold
on to this and read it later?' He fingered it appreciatively.
'It feels nice and thick.'

Celia hurtled around a corner with unnecessarily
violence.

'Quite all right,' I assured him, deciding not to
mention the earlier letter. 'You can give it back when
you're finished with it.'

'Here we are—' Celia slammed on the brakes. She
glared at her oblivious husband. 'This is where you get
off!'

'Oh, yes, thanks.' Patrick got out, displaying more
animation that I had yet seen in him. 'And thank you,
Rosemary, thanks a lot.'

'Don't bother doing supper for us,' Celia snapped.
'We'll eat in Boston.' She sent him a deadly smile. 'That
will give you more time to write to Nancy.'

'Good idea.' He was left staring after us blankly as we
roared away.

The children didn't seem to have noticed anything, so I
held my peace. In any case, I knew better than to cross
Celia when she was in this sort of mood. I was surprised,
though. I had had the impression that she and Nancy
were good friends. It was beginning to look as though all
the friendship was on Patrick's side—and bitterly
resented by Celia.

We drove through town in silence, except for the
prattle of the children. Just before we reached the turn
for the main highway, Celia slowed down.

'I just have to run in here for a minute.' She pulled up

in front of the Singletons' antique shop. 'It won't take
long.'

'Oh, good.' I started to get out. 'I haven't seen this
place yet. I've been wanting to—'

'Can we come too?' Tessa and Timothy tried to crowd
out behind me.

'You can all wait here!' Celia snapped. 'There are too
many of us. The shop isn't big enough.' She reached over
and took a small wrapped parcel from the glove compartment before getting out. 'And it's the kind of place—' she
warned me—'where, if you break anything, you've
bought it.'

'You'd better stay here,' I told Tessa and Timothy. 'We
won't be long.'

Celia gave me a venomous look and I smiled at her
blandly. 'Don't worry,' I said. 'I won't break anything.'

The shop bell tinkled as we opened the door and
stepped inside. I was immediately glad that we had left
the children in the car. It was one of those artfully-
cluttered places, lacking only fake cobwebs sprayed in
corners, that set warning bells ringing at the back of one's
mind. Viv and Hank would know the placement of every
item to the fraction of a millimetre and the cost of
breakage would be excessively high.

'Hi, there—' Viv emerged from a room at the rear of
the shop and came forward beaming. 'You finally made
it!' she greeted me, while her eyes slid sideways to the
parcel in Celia's hand.

'Sorry it took so long,' I told her. 'But I'm here now.'

'Wonderful!' She couldn't care less. Long experience
had undoubtedly taught her the difference between a
buyer and a browser. A seller, however, was another
matter. She transferred her welcoming smile to Celia,
allowing a slight pre-bargaining chill to creep into it, but
she could not hide the acquisitive gleam in her eyes.

'I'd like to speak to you for a minute—' Celia was not

prepared to waste time. 'If my sister will excuse us.'

'Don't bother about me,' I said. 'I'm quite content to browse.'

'Certainly.' Viv answered us both, a certain sardonic tilt of one eyebrow betraying that I had answered as expected. She continued to look with favour on me, however. Celia's home was a storehouse of potential profit; who knew what goldmine her sister might possess back in England?

Not even I knew that. Nor would I know until Nancy and her tribe had finished their dilapidations and I got home to see what had been left intact.

Celia and Viv disappeared into the back and I heard a brief murmur of voices before the door was firmly closed. With a mental shrug, I began my browsing.

After I had picked up the thistle-etched Jacobean drinking glass and looked at the price, I didn't pick up anything else. My fingers had gone quite weak at the sight and I didn't want to tempt Providence. I contented myself with twisting my head to try to read the price tags; those I could decipher made me feel increasingly giddy. The more exclusive items were priced in code, still others were unpriced: the universal code for *If you have to ask, you can't afford it*.

I moved over to the other side of the shop where an opulently unobtrusive butler's tray and stand held a selection of delicate porcelain. It took me a moment to realize what I was looking at.

The set of Four Seasons figurines, the Lalique lamp—even the butler's tray itself—were all too familiar. The last time I had seen them—apart from photographs—was when I had helped Celia to pack them.

It was no more than I had suspected, but it was still disconcerting. Previously I had felt guilty for harbouring such suspicions, now I felt worse for having proved them. With Celia right in the next room, too.

I moved away rapidly before she could return and discover me discovering her. It was just as well I did. I had hardly reached the neutral zone of Early American milk glass when the door at the rear of the shop opened and Celia and Viv came back to join me.

'See anything you can't resist?' Viv asked archly.

'Not really,' I smiled. 'I'm afraid it's all too rich for my blood.'

'You mustn't tempt her now, Viv,' Celia scolded. 'We're on our way to Boston for a shopping spree.' Unconsciously she patted her handbag with a little smile of satisfaction. 'We're looking for clothes this trip.'

'You'll find them. The stores will be unloading their summer lines now to make way for the Fall stock. I wish I could come with you, but Hank's off on a buying tour and someone has to keep the home fires burning.'

I glanced at her sharply, but she appeared unaware of any double entendre in what she had just said. Probably it had been said in all innocence, but if I were one of the native inhabitants of Edgemarsh Lake, I'd be a bit more careful about my language these days.

'Come on.' Celia nudged me forward. 'The kids will be getting restless.'

'Have fun,' Viv called after us.

'There!' Celia said, as the screen door swung shut behind us. 'That's a good job done. I've been bored with those old miniatures for years and Viv's been longing to get her hands on them.'

'Oh, Celia—not those lovely "After Gainsboroughs"?!'

'I'm planning to redecorate,' Celia said firmly, 'and they won't go with my new colour scheme. Besides, Viv finally made me an offer too good to refuse. Mind you, she'll get a lot more than that for them, even though she has to send them to her New York shop to do it. There just isn't that sort of money around here any more.'

'It does seem a shame.' Celia had always maintained

that the beauty of paintings was that they transcended
colour schemes. However, it was done and there was no
point arguing.

'I'll pick up more interesting pictures on my next trip
over,' Celia said defiantly. 'Meanwhile, I've got a windfall
that will provide new wardrobes for the whole family,
with more than enough left over for me to treat us to a
slap-up meal in Boston. And all for a couple of boring old
miniatures I've long since grown tired of looking at!'

'How super!' I could hardly call her a liar. I wondered
just how bad the financial position was. There were too
many telltale dark patches on her walls, too many
treasures missing from their assigned places.

Had Hank and Viv ('our friendly local scavengers,'
Pixie had called them) siphoned away the lot? Or had
they been dispersed, piece by piece, among several eager
buyers?

Probably no one would ever know. Celia had had to
admit it this time because I was right there with her as she
went to sell the miniatures. She sounded pretty sure of
their eventual destination, so the process was evidently
familiar to her. Undoubtedly, Viv and Hank despatched
most of their purchases to New York with the dual
purpose of getting more money and saving Celia's face.
Perhaps Celia made the stipulation herself, so that no
local residents carelessly browsing through the shop might
recognize the items and thus guess how difficult her
financial position had become.

Had Patrick lost his job as well as his health? He was
home far too often—even for a top salesman with
complete autonomy over his territory and his schedule.

'Furthermore—' Celia gave a final cheery wave to Viv
and slid behind the steering-wheel—'we'll stop at Captain
Ahab's again and have ice cream for elevenses!'

Boston had the fascination of the old and the new

jumbled together, each holding its own better than might have been expected. The imposing skyscrapers dwarfed but did not diminish the dignity of the State House, with its goldleaf dome, looking down over the green sweep of Boston Common to the red brick of Park Street Church with its gleaming white steeple.

We plunged into the basements of the big stores— Filene's and Jordan Marsh—and ransacked them for bargains. We did so well that we had to return to the parking lot and lock our bundles into the boot of the car before returning—this time to the upstairs departments—for more booty.

Celia spent wildly—perhaps desperately. Was it an attempt to convince me that she had no financial troubles? Or was it simply the spending spree of a woman who had counted her pennies for far too long and needed to break out or break down?

From the big stores, we went to the smaller shops. We bore away books, costume jewellery, postcards, jigsaw puzzles, a tea-set Tessa fell in love with, a spaceman's outfit—against my better judgement—for Timothy, and so many small items that we promptly forgot them and were amazed to discover them later.

'I'm shopped out,' Celia sighed happily. 'My back is breaking, my feet are killing me—and I don't want to see Boston again for another six months.'

'It will take them that long to restock,' Luke said, and nimbly dodged the loaded shopping-bag his mother swung at his legs.

'One more trip to the car to dump all this,' Celia proposed, 'and then we'll find something to eat.'

The evening rush hour was upon us by the time we had disposed of our packages. We joined the stream heading towards the harbour. We poured through the pedestrian precincts by City Hall and the stream divided and subdivided again, some veering off for the multi-storied car

parks to reclaim their vehicles, some crossing to the bus
station at Haymarket Square for their coaches to the
outer suburbs and commuter towns along the North
Shore.

'We're going to Quincy Market,' Celia said, leading us
across a street and into a cobblestoned area of thriving
activity. 'This has all been done up in recent years—' she
waved a hand at the low buildings housing shops, ice
cream parlours, restaurants, food shops and workshops
for craftspeople. 'It's a great tourist attraction and most
of the local residents like it, too.'

'It looks like a Bostonian version of Covent Garden,' I
decided as we strolled around. Beyond us, the deep blue
harbour sparkled in the sun. 'Is that—?'

'The very same. Farther up, they have a Tea Party Ship
and Museum. You can still throw tea chests in the
harbour, and they're retrieved by rope harnesses. But it's
all done in good fun these days. Except for the time the
Russians shot down that Korean civilian jetliner—then
some people came and threw cases of vodka into Boston
Harbour. It was the beginning of the boycott on vodka.'

'I never heard about that.'

'Oh, there are lots of things you don't hear about from
one country to another.'

Including, of course, family financial problems.
However, by this time, I was too hungry to worry about
lesser things. Fragrant aromas drifted out from the
restaurants and our steps slowed as we debated the
delicious choices. The children voted for the one
featuring the most spectacular desserts and we settled
ourselves at a table and ordered.

By the time we had finished our meal, it was dark and a
bright moon was lighting the Market. Music and laughter
carried on the cool breeze sweeping in from the ocean; it
seemed a perfect night.

'We'll stop at a bakery,' Celia said to Luke, 'and pick

up something nice for Daddy.' Suddenly I was swept by an aching sadness because there was no one waiting for us. No one but Errol.

'We've got a lovely kitty-bag for Errol,' Timothy said stoutly. The children must have felt it, too.

'Wait till he sees it,' Tessa said, blinking valiantly. 'He'll be so excited.'

'Errol will be delighted to see us,' I agreed. He was about to be the happy recipient of two Italian meatballs, two pork chop bones with plenty of meat and fat on them and two butterfly shrimp. Perhaps it would be wise to close the living-room door before we went upstairs tonight.

The atmosphere changed as we walked away from Quincy Market. The way back to the parking lot led through the now-deserted business district. Away from the harbour, there was no coolness in the air. Dark unsettling shadows moved in darker doorways. I repressed a scream as one of them lurched across the pavement ahead of us.

'Street people,' Celia said softly. 'Patrick always says there's no harm in them, but they frighten me, too.'

I pulled the children closer to me. Possibly there was no real harm in the sad derelicts, but they seemed more menacing at night.

'Here we are—' There was relief in Celia's voice. We turned into the parking lot, glad to see that it was well-lighted and had an attendant. We piled into the car thankfully and headed back to New Hampshire.

The children had carried the first load of shopping into the house at Cranberry Lane and I was unloading more from the trunk, when Celia suddenly caught my arm.

'Rosemary—' Shadows moved across her face, she looked as furtive and out of place as the street people for a moment. "Could I ask you a favour?'

'Of course.'

'My shopping—' She indicated the mound of parcels belonging to her. 'I'm afraid I went overboard. Patrick will have a fit if he sees it all. Could you keep it here for me until I have a chance to break it gently to him? Or perhaps I could smuggle it into the house bit by bit. I don't want to upset him.'

'Of course.' What else could I say? 'Bring it in and we'll find a cupboard for it until you want it.'

I was glad that the moon had gone behind a cloud and she could not see my face. She didn't want Patrick to know how much money she had spent. Because they couldn't afford it? Or because he would ask where she had found it?

Was she selling the antiques without Patrick's knowledge?

CHAPTER 14

It was as well we hadn't postponed our shopping spree in the hope of better weather. The next day was even hotter and the day after that unbearable. Then the temperature settled down in the low 90's for the next week and seemed about to remain there for the rest of the summer.

'We need a good thunderstorm to clear the air,' Celia complained. 'I've never known it so bad. And it's not August yet—that's supposed to be the worst month. That's when we have what they call the "dog days", when dogs are supposed to go mad from the heat. People, too—the murder rate always goes up during August.'

'Wonderful!' My own temper was beginning to fray. 'Do you have any more good news?'

'Patrick has had a letter from Nancy.' For a moment I thought she had taken my question seriously, then I noticed her expression. She did not consider that good news, it was part of her catalogue of complaints. 'Nancy says the weather is mild and damp over there and she's having a wonderful time.'

'I'm pleased to hear it. Have they smashed up anything else lately?'

'She didn't say. At least, I don't think she said. I haven't seen the letter. Patrick just read out bits to me.'

I glanced at her sharply. Was there something a little too evasive about that reply?

'Poor Errol,' Celia changed the subject quickly. 'This weather is hard on him, too.' Errol was lying in the shadiest corner of the veranda, looking as wilted as the plants. We were lazing on the swing with a pitcher of iced lemonade, waiting until it was time to drive over to Camp and collect the children.

'He hasn't even gone out prowling the past few nights,' I agreed. 'He wants to stay indoor with the air-conditioning.' I had given up that struggle. We had begun by turning it on for an hour or two each day to cool the house, now we kept it on most of the time. I was developing a double guilt complex: first, because we were running up Nancy's electricity bill; second, because the electric company itself was now placing large advertisement in all the newspapers asking people to conserve electricity lest there be more of a demand than the grid could handle and another big blackout ensue.

'It can't go on much longer,' Celia said unconvincingly.

'It's gone on far too long already. The lake is inches lower than it was when we arrived and—' I didn't want to finish the thought.

'And the woods are parched,' Celia completed it for me. Involuntarily we both glanced towards the dry rustling pines. They'd go up like torches at the slightest spark.

'I'm glad Greg has banned campfires,' I said. I still had

reservations about Camp Mohigonquin but had convinced myself that my imagination had been working overtime the night we dined at Gino's Place. At any rate, I had no concrete excuse for denying the children the amenities of the camp and I continued to allow them to attend.

'Oh, he's very careful.' Celia deposited her cigarette ash in the deep bowl she was using in place of the shallow ashtray; she was being very careful, too. 'The danger is some tourist smoking carelessly. Most of them are from cities and don't realize that they can't throw away lighted cigarette stubs here the way they do on city streets. That's why we have warning signs at the entrance to the woods. Chief Rogers fines them on the spot if he catches them doing it.'

'So he should. It would be better if people didn't smoke at all—at least until the danger is over.' This was a delicate subject. The anti-smoking faction in America was so vociferous—not to say downright objection-able—that smokers were becoming a persecuted minority. I smoked an occasional cigarette myself, but had to feel concern at the amount Celia was smoking. They couldn't be doing her any good. Of course, she was going through a difficult time and I recognized that she needed every crutch available. I suppose I could only be thankful that she hadn't taken to drink the way she had taken to cigarettes.

'Rosemary—' Celia was on her feet suddenly, staring into the woods. 'Do you smell smoke?'

'We've probably talked ourselves into it.' But I joined her at the railing. 'I don't think . . . wait a minute . . . I'm not sure.'

A thin grey spiral snaked into the sky in the distance.

'There!' Celia pointed to it but I had already seen it.

Errol got up and came over to stand at our feet. He lifted his head and sniffed, his whiskers twitched uneasily.

That made it unanimous.

A second, thicker, grey spiral drifted up and merged with the first.

'What's over there?' I asked.

'I'm trying to think—distances are deceptive. There are summer cottages dotted all through the woods. Log cabins, most of them. And all along the Mohigonquin Trail there are wooden huts where hikers can shelter for the night or from the rain. The rain—' She scanned the sky hopelessly. The only cloud in sight was the rapidly growing cloud of smoke over the forest.

'We'd better report it!' Celia whirled and dashed into the house, heading for the telephone.

Errol stirred and crouched to jump down from the veranda.

'Oh no you don't!' I pounced on him and caught him up. 'You're not going wandering in the woods right now. You're coming into the house and staying there!' I carried him inside.

Celia was just replacing the receiver as the Fire Whistle in town began blasting out its grim message. Automatically I began counting silently.

'They'd just had a report from a Park Ranger,' Celia said. 'He'd spotted it from his lookout tower. But it's better to have too many people reporting it than no one at all.'

There had been a pause, now the series of blasts began again. This time Celia stood silent and counted with me.

'Four—' She turned to me with fear in her eyes. 'That's North! The Camp is North! If they can't contain the fire, if it spreads through the woods—' Suddenly she was running. I was right behind her.

The whoop of sirens sounded along the town road as we leaped into the car and Celia started the engine. It sounded as though they were sending out all their engines again. Even so, they'd be lucky if they could get enough of

the woods immediately surrounding the blaze wetted
down before the flames took hold.

We careered out into the main highway. Celia was
taking no account of speed limits and I was not going to
remind her of them. The children were more important.

She drove so fast that we caught up with the engines in
time to see them veer off on the fork that led into the
North woods.

There were more clouds ahead of us now. For a
moment, I was afraid the fire had started in a new
location, then the clouds wheeled and circled and I
realized they were flocks of birds driven out of the woods
by the encroaching danger and flying to refuge elsewhere.

'Thank heavens there's no wind,' Celia said. 'This is the
first time all summer I've been thankful there isn't a
breeze.'

'The fire seems a good distance away,' I said. 'And
there's the highway dividing the two sides of the woods.'

'Don't build any hopes on that.' Celia's mouth was a
tight grim line. 'Fire jumps, you know.'

I knew, but I had been repressing the knowledge. We
swung into the turning for Camp Mohigonquin and the
clouds were behind us. Out of sight, but never out of
mind.

The camp seemed strangely peaceful when we reached
it after our wild dash. The campers were gathered on the
hillside sweeping down to the lake, watching something
that was happening on the shoreline.

'There they are!' I spotted Tessa and Timothy,
standing with Luke and Dexter, and felt the knot of
tension in my stomach begin to loosen. They were safe.
They had not decided to go for any hikes in the woods.
They were placidly standing on the hillside watching the
Sailing Club preparing for its races.

'Leave them there a minute.' Celia's grip was tight on
my arm. 'We'd better find Greg and have a quiet word.

He'll know whether any of the kids have gone hiking in the woods.'

It looked as though the whole camp had turned out for the races, but we had to make sure. The children hadn't seen us, so we moved away quietly. Greg wasn't in sight; he was probably in the Administration Building.

The building was empty. We checked the Cookhouse and the Dispensary, but they were also deserted. Everyone must be out watching the races.

'He must be down on the shore, after all,' Celia said. 'Let's go back.'

Our sense of urgency had abated. Obviously the races were too big an event for any camper to miss. It was most unlikely that any of the children would have taken themselves off to the woods with them in prospect.

Benjie, the new Counsellor, seemed to be the kingpin of the Sailing Club. He was everywhere, giving directions, lending a hand to launch a boat, trying to line up the entries. We had to speak to him three times before he noticed we were there.

'I know Lois went into town to do an errand, but Greg's around somewhere. . . . Huh? Yeah, sure all the kids are here. Why wouldn't they be?' He paused and a thoughtful look came into his eyes. 'Unless—'

By then our own children had spotted us and came running down the hill.

'Yeah, all present and accounted for.' Benjie gave a satisfied nod. 'The only one ever likely to go missing is Dexter, but here he is.'

'Mummy—' Tessa slid her hand into mine. 'You're early. Did you come to see the races?'

'There's Greg!' Celia cut across Tessa's question. Greg had appeared at the top of the hill, coming from the direction of the camp buildings. 'Where was he? We looked everywhere.'

'Not quite,' I reminded her. 'Neither of us looked into the Gents.'

'That's so.' She started towards him, to intercept him before he got within earshot of the campers.

'I'll be right back—' I slipped out of Tessa's grasp. 'You stay here, we just want to talk to Greg for a minute.'

'Hi, folks,' Greg greeted us. 'Come to see the races?'

His expression changed radically as we told him why we had come.

'Well, hell!' He looked around the camp, rapidly taking a mental tally. 'That's one Chief Rogers can't pin on us. Everybody's here. No way could any of my gang be responsible.'

I wondered if Chief Rogers would take that view. The kids might all be here now—but where had they been an hour or so ago? Rumour had it that the investigators had found a timing device in the ruins of the Old Tithe Barn. An alibi for any particular moment no long meant anything.

'It could have been spontaneous combustion,' Celia said. Her tone suggested that she didn't really believe it. 'The woods are so dry now.'

'Anyway,' Greg said comfortably, 'it sounds as though the Park Ranger spotted it in time—and you, too, of course. If the engines can get through without too much trouble, we're in with a fighting chance.'

Below us, a starting gun was fired and the small boats straggled out from the wharf to the cheers of onlooking friends.

'We thought—' Celia said carefully—'we'd come and collect the children.'

'Now—and ruin their day?' Greg was indignant. 'They've been looking forward to the races all week. Honest, there's no danger. Even if there were, they'd be safer here where they can always dive into the lake. What could be safer than that?'

'That may be all right for the others.' I voiced my fears. 'But Tessa's arm won't be out of the cast for another week. I wouldn't rate her chances very highly if she had to swim for it.' Tessa was an inexpert swimmer at the best of times.

'Oh, we'd load the non-swimmers into the boats with the provisions—' He broke off abruptly, realizing that he was arguing along the wrong tack and started again. 'I mean, I take your point, I really do. And I don't blame you for being jumpy. But, I promise you, everything is going to be okay.

'Look—I'll tell you what I'll do. We'll go back to Admin and I'll telephone the lookout tower for the latest report.' He turned and led us back to the buildings. 'Come on, you can speak to him yourselves.'

'Yes, ma'am,' the Park Ranger said patiently. 'I've been keeping my binoculars on the fire all along. I'm happy to say the firemen appear to have achieved a containment situation. They're going in on the main blaze now and should have it under control soon. There's absolutely no danger over where you are. Have a nice day.' He rang off.

'You see?' Greg was relieved and cautiously triumphant. 'Now, why don't you come down and watch the races? When they're over, it will be time for the day kids to go home anyway.'

'All right.' We fell into step beside him, still brooding. There was a faint trace of smoke drifting on the air. Celia sniffed sharply.

'I'll tell you what,' Greg placated. 'As soon as Lois gets back, I'll set her to sorting out some emergency rations and we'll stack them in the boathouse. Then, if anything happens, we can load the boats with the rations and the non-swimmers and push out from shore. If necessary, we could ride it out in the middle of the lake for three or four days.'

It was not the comforting prospect he seemed to imagine. The thought of Tessa and Timothy in a small boat on a lake ringed with fire made me clench my fists until my nails bit into my palms. I told myself to keep calm. These people faced the hazards of forest fires every time they had a drought. Surely they must know the best way of dealing with it.

Celia made an indeterminate dubious sound; I knew she was picturing Luke in the same circumstances. No, we were not the least bit comforted or reassured.

The children came forward to pull us towards the edge of the lake, pointing out their favourites among the boats. Celia and I exchanged a glance of reluctant accord: we would not spoil the occasion by frightening the children. We would stay and cheer the races, but be ready to move if danger seemed to threaten.

As the afternoon wore on without mishap, we relaxed slightly, no longer turning so often to scan the horizon for betraying wisps of smoke. The air seemed clearer, the hint of smoke had dissipated. A small breeze seemed to be springing up off the lake. It was not so welcome as it would have been this morning. The long triumphant blasts signalling that the fire was out still had not sounded. We weren't out of the woods yet—and neither was the fire.

The staring gun went for the final race of the afternoon. The races had gone on a little too long to keep their audience enthralled. Some of the campers had already drifted away; others were growing restive.

'You don't happen to have a chocolate bar on you, do you?' Dexter wheedled hopefully.

'If I did have, it would have long since melted in this heat,' I pointed out practically. 'How about a peppermint?'

'Aw, I'm starving.' He took the peppermint, it was better than nothing. 'Thanks.'

'You'll be eating soon, won't you?'

'Yeah.' He made a face. 'If you can call it that. Usually we roast hot dogs after the races and sit around the campfire and sing songs. But Greg won't let us have any fires now. So we're going to have boring old boiled hot dogs—at least when you cook them over a campfire, the scorching adds a bit of zing.'

And, under cover of darkness, the Counsellors could not keep count of his intake.

'That's too bad,' I said. 'I'm afraid you'll just have to tell yourself that you can't have Steak Diane every night.'

'When I'm grown up I can.' His eyes gleamed greedily. 'I'll eat in all the best restaurants and eat everything I want. Once I'm of age, nobody can stop me. I'll have Steak Diane, crêpes Suzette, bananas flambé . . .'

Every dish requiring flickering flames. I looked away uneasily lest he catch the thought. Was Dexter a gourmet or a pyromaniac?

I didn't want to think that Dexter was the arsonist, but he certainly had quite a few earmarks of the breed. Nor could I exonerate him from suspicion on the grounds that the mechanics of delayed action devices might be too complicated for him. Adolescents these days had a level of technical achievement that left adults standing.

A burst of cheering brought me back to reality. The last race had been won.

'Thank heavens,' Celia breathed. 'Now we can go.'

As we mounted the crest of the hill, a police car was pulling to a stop outside the Administration Building. I was suddenly thankful that the children had lingered at the shore to help a friend beach his boat.

Chief Rogers got out of the car and looked around, frowning.

'Now, see here—' Greg came striding out of the cookhouse to meet him, with a face like a thundercloud. 'You can't pin this one on Camp Mohigonquin. Every one

of my campers has been here all day. We've never been
out of each other's sights. This time you're going to have
to stop trying to take the easy way out and go and find the
real firebug.'

'Oh, Chief Rogers,' Celia stepped between them
quickly. 'Do you have any news? Is the fire out? Was it one
of the log cabins or is it in the woods?'

'Hello, Miz Meadows.' The chief acknowledged her
while ignoring Greg. 'No, it's not out yet, but the boys
have it pretty much under control. It was one of the
Hikers' Shelters on the Old Mohigonquin Trail.' He shook
his head. 'Won't nobody be sheltering there again in a
hurry.'

'My campers had nothing to do with it,' Greg insisted.

'Sure of that, are you?' Captain Rogers turned cold eyes
on him.

'Positive.' Greg met his eyes with equal coldness. 'Half
the kids have been out on the lake all afternoon, the other
half have been watching them. You can ask these ladies
here, if you don't believe me. There's no way you can link
that fire with anyone at this camp.'

'Maybe just one way.' Chief Rogers reached into his hip
pocket and drew out a folded handkerchief; he peeled
back the folds carefully. 'Recognize this, do you?' A small
charred object on a blackened chain was exposed to view.

'Why, uh, I don't know . . .' Greg bent closer. 'It sort of
looks like . . .' He began shaking his head.

'Like what?' Chief Rogers prompted.

'Uh . . . just vaguely . . . like that jade frog Lois wears
around her neck. Oh no—you can't think that. Not Lois!
That's even crazier than suspecting the kids. No. She
must have lost it. I mean—long ago. Or—or it's been
planted by someone with a grudge against Camp
Mohigonquin. Lois would never have started those fires.'

'Maybe not.' Chief Rogers covered the frog again and
replaced it in his pocket. 'Do you think I could speak to

the lady? I'd kinda like to ask her a few questions.'

'Sure,' Greg said. 'No, wait. She went into town on some errand. She's not back yet—Oh, listen—she wouldn't run out on us. She'd have no reason to. I promise you, there's some good explanation. She's as innocent as the rest of us.'

'Ay-yuh,' Chief Rogers sighed. He did not seem in any hurry to put out an alarm on a missing suspect. He stared out over the lake sadly.

'Listen,' Greg said. 'Listen, where did you find that . . . that thing?'

'There was a body in the shelter. The chain was around its neck.'

'No! No, listen—it couldn't have been Lois! Look, she's due back any minute. She went into town. There'll be some explanation. What you're thinking is impossible. What would she be doing in a shelter on the trail? There was no reason for her to go up there.'

I could think of a reason: she might have gone up there to meet someone. My eyes blurred with tears. Poor Lois. She was never going to find that Prince, after all.

'Ay-yuh.' Chief Rogers sighed again. 'You don't happen to know the name of her dentist, do you?'

CHAPTER 15

That night I sat for a long time in the rocking-chair by the open window, fighting sleep. *What dreams must come* I did not want to face, nor the even more painful moments of awakening to find that they had been but dreams.

A fitful breeze danced through the smouldering woods bringing the scent of smoke through the screen window. *If worst comes to worst*, Chief Rogers had told us, we would be evacuated from our homes in good time before the fire reached them. We would be asked to take only our most precious—and portable—possessions with us.

But it was not my house, it was Nancy's. What would she most want to be saved? Usually the sentimental items were the most valued. What did I know of her private life and the things she most cherished? I could only guess.

Errol, of course. There was no question about that. He was curled up on my lap, purring loudly and apparently resigned to the fact that, for some mysterious reason, he was not going to be allowed out of the house tonight. He had used his indoor litter box with a couple of bitter complaints, then followed me upstairs to leap into my lap, graciously forgiving me.

We would have ample warning to evacuate, Chief Rogers had assured us. But would we? If that errant breeze were to stiffen into a high wind, fanning the smouldering ashes and sweeping the fire before it?

What if another fire were to be started? In another part of the woods—somewhere closer? There was no doubt now that we had an arsonist in the community. An arsonist—and a murderer.

A multiple murderer. Those two still-unidentified hikers had been the first victims, probably just because they had been in the wrong place at the wrong time. Lois's death was more sinister. The fact that she had been found in a place she would not normally have gone near, after having started out for some other place, gave rise to another question. Had she died because she would have been able to identify the arsonist?

There were flickering lights in the distance. I leaned forward, peering towards them intently. Errol gave a muffled cry of protest at being squashed and I soothed him absently.

Heat lightning? We had had that several times, giving rise to false hopes of a thunderstorm and a saving downpour which never materialized. Perhaps the Aurora Borealis? It was not an unknown phenomenon in this region.

Not fire. Please God not fire.

The low rumble of thunder answered me and I fell back against the chair limply. The chair immediately began a wild rocking. Errol protested again.

'All right, all right.' I cuddled him, comforting myself as much as him. 'It's all right . . . this time.'

At some point, I must have dozed. I had been dreaming, another dream I could not quite recapture as it dissolved into the mists, but it had been ended by what I had learned to recognize as the nightmare *finale* of all my dreams: the sound of a coffin lid falling.

I opened my eyes, momentarily disorientated, conscious that something was peculiar and extraordinarily unsettling. I was still sitting up in the rocking-chair. Errol was poised, hind feet on my lap, front paws on the window seat, looking out alertly, far more awake than I.

I blinked at him, still trying to shake off the dream phantoms still clinging round me. Then Errol's attitude registered. That, and the way he turned his head questioningly towards me.

Errol had heard it, too!

He was a smart cat, but not smart enough to tune in on my dreams. There *had* been a noise somewhere outside, a hollow thud I had transmuted into the sound of a coffin lid falling. I wondered: just in this dream—or in all of them?

I lifted Errol to one side and stood up, raising the screen and leaning out of the window. The air was hot and breathless, the breeze had disappeared. So had the moon. There was no sound now but the small normal night sounds.

Could it have been a shot? Some hunter in the woods after rabbits or squirrels? Or, illegally, because the season had not yet opened, hunting deer? Or was it someone hunting quite different prey?

It couldn't be our avowed friend and nearest neighbour prowling around trying to catch Errol again, could it? I wouldn't put it past him. Noah Peterson might have dropped a trap he was carrying—or some sort of box he had intended to hold Errol.

That reminded me. I must look around for Errol's carrying case. If we had to evacuate in a hurry, I didn't want to try to cope with a struggling cat in my arms. There must be one somewhere around for him.

Meanwhile, whoever or whatever had been outside, it was there no longer. I lowered the screen thoughtfully and turned away from the window.

I awoke with a headache which the baking heat did nothing to alleviate. The children were fractious and argumentative. They could see no reason why they should not attend camp as usual. The television promised that the fire was under control, even though it could not be extinguished, and was being monitored by firemen and Park Rangers. The weather forecast held out a half-hearted hope of relief soon. I had the impression that the hope was offered more as an encouragement to morale than an accurate prediction of conditions.

Celia rang to see what I was doing and was not in the sweetest of moods herself. Luke also considered a little thing like a forest fire a poor excuse for missing camp.

'It's this Benjie,' Celia complained. 'He's promised to start giving archery lessons today and Luke is frantic to learn.'

That also explained why Timothy was so keen to be there today, and Tessa was determined not to be left out of any excitement.

'We might as well let them go,' Celia said. 'They'll have to hear about Lois sooner or later and it will be easier for them if they're with the others when they hear. Peer Group support is very important at these times.'

'Mm-hmm,' I said, thinking that Celia sounded completely Americanized at times.

'And frankly,' Celia's voice was shaky, 'I'd rather not be the one to tell Luke about Lois. Let him pick it up at camp where he'll have the other kids to help him handle it. It will be easier for Tessa and Timothy that way, too. And you.'

She was right. If I broke it to the children, it would inevitably become entwined in their minds with their memories of their father's death; whereas, if they learned about it at camp, it would simply be another incomprehensible event in a strange and bewildering summer.

And Celia had her own reasons for not wanting to break any more bad news than was necessary to Luke.

'I'll collect Tessa and Timothy, then,' Celia said. 'Why don't you come along and we'll go to Nashua after we leave them off? We can have lunch there and explore.'

'Not today,' I told her. 'I have a raging headache. I just want a quiet day.'

'It would do you good to get out and forget about it.' Celia sounded affronted. 'Take a couple of aspirin and come along.'

'Sorry, Celia, I'd rather not.'

'I think you're being silly.' It was not like Celia to argue so much. I wondered what she had really planned for us to do in Nashua.

'Anyway,' I said, 'Pixie Toller is coming over later this morning. I've told her I'll be here.' It was not strictly true, Pixie had only said that she might drop by, but it sufficed to satisfy Celia.

'Oh, very well,' she said, with bad grace. 'Why didn't you say so at the beginning?'

'Because I honestly do have a headache—' I was talking to the dialling tone. Celia had rung off.

CONSERVE ENERGY—The headline of the advertisement screamed at me. I turned the page. DO NOT USE HOSEPIPES OR SPRINKLER SYSTEMS. YOU CAN BE FINED UP TO $200.00.

I was getting that feeling of a giant elbow in my ribs again. Even the news headline had been: WOODS CLOSED TO CAMPERS AND HIKERS UNTIL FURTHER NOTICE.

A car drove past as I looked up. The bumper sticker read: HAVE YOU HUGGED YOUR KIDS TODAY? Even the State licence plates exhorted: LIVE FREE OR DIE.

I was not in the best of moods when Pixie arrived. She looked around the veranda critically.

'Have you been talking to the plants?'

'No,' I said defiantly. 'But I've had several meaningful discussions with Errol lately.'

'Errol doesn't count. It's too easy to talk to him. He answers back. Errol will always be all right, but I don't know what Nancy's going to say if she comes home and finds all her hanging baskets have died. She always talked to them for ten minutes every morning. They're pining for her.'

'This State,' I said coldly, 'is in the middle of the worst heat wave and drought in recorded history. There's no water to spare and everything is parched and burning up. I very much doubt that a few kind words will do anything to change that situation.'

'You don't have to conserve that much water,' Pixie said., 'No one will mind if you water the house plants.' She lowered one of the hanging baskets and gazed into it.

'Poor little thing,' she cooed. 'You miss your mother, don't you? And your poor little roots are all dry and gasping for moisture. Here—' she tipped her glass into the basket. 'Aunt Pixie will give you her own lemonade to drink and then you'll feel a lot better.'

I watched incredulously. It was hard to believe that this

was the same woman who was plagued by violent dreams which betrayed the seething mass of hatred deep within her.

'There—' She swung the basket up again and hitched the cord around the hook in the pillar. 'Now I'll just get some water and take care of the rest—'

'Don't let Errol out!' I blocked him with my foot as he tried to sneak past when the screen door opened.

'What's the matter?' She returned with a jug of water. 'Has he been a bad boy—as usual?'

'No. It's just that I don't feel it's safe for him to be out in the woods with that fire still burning. If it should get out of control and we have to leave in a hurry, I want him where we can pick him up and take him with us.'

'Yes,' Pixie said thoughtfully. 'That's a bad scene. Did you hear the latest?' Pixie would always have the latest—accurate or not. 'They say that girl was strangled before the fire was started. So she couldn't have set it.'

'I never thought she had.'

'I guess none of us did, really. It's just that it was more comfortable to think that, maybe, she was the firebug and got hoist by her own petard. Only now—' Pixie shuddered—'it looks like she caught him starting the fire and he strangled her.'

I watched Pixie's strong capable hands as she raised the last basket and lashed the cord, pulling it a little too tightly. The flash of suspicion was momentary, but it shook me. Was this what we were coming to—suspecting each other?

'So now we have to look elsewhere,' Pixie continued, unaware that I already had. 'But I hate to think it could have been somebody from the town. Or one of the kids from Camp—' She looked at me and glanced away quickly.

It was the first time I realized that the Blake Family might come under suspicion. We were unknown, foreign, with only Celia—who was, after all, another foreigner—to vouch for our background. How did anyone know that I was all right? That Timothy had not been in trouble with the Juvenile Authorities at home? Or how Tessa had really broken her arm? Once suspicion began to infiltrate a community, there was no end to it.

'One thing I've been meaning to tell you,' Pixie said hastily, as though to make amends. 'If we *do* have to get out in a hurry, I'll come round with the Welcome Wagon and get you and the kids. I'm nearer than Celia and we may have to move fast. Tell Celia we'll meet them at the Emergency Center.'

'Oh, thank you—' I'd been worried about that. Celia was half way around the lake and the fire might cut us off.

'It probably won't come to that,' Pixie said. 'There are a couple of emergency measures they'll take first. They haven't even dynamited a fire-break yet. It may never happen.'

'I know,' I said. 'But it's the thought that . . . out there . . . the woods are still burning . . . and there's nothing we can do . . .'

'We can pray for rain,' Pixie said. 'That's what I've been doing all week. I've gone into every Church—of whatever denomination—for miles around and said a prayer. And just in case—' She glanced at me obliquely. 'I've got a book from the library and tonight I'm going to do the Mohigonquin Rain Dance. You never know—it was their territory, after all.'

'I suppose it can't do any harm.' I carefully refrained from saying whether I thought it would do any good.

'There's a full moon tonight, too. That's supposed to be heap big medicine.'

It was also supposed to bring out the nut-cases in force. Again, I felt it would be more tactful not to comment.

'It would be even better,' Pixie said wistfully, 'if I could

do the dance on the old Sacred Ground. Only that's right
by the back door of the Peterson house. I'm not sure
Noah would—'

'Noah Peterson is another reason I don't want Errol
roaming free right now.' I grasped the opportunity to
change the subject. 'I'm afraid Noah is on the prowl
again.' I had already told her about his obsession. 'I'd
thought we'd arranged a truce, but now it seems he was
just trying to lull me into a false sense of security. He's still
after Errol.'

'That Peterson family has always been pretty odd.'
Serenely, she called the kettle black. 'You never can tell
about them. It could be. Once they get an idea into their
heads, they don't give it up easily.'

'Mrs Blake—Rosemary—' Perhaps I should not have been
surprised when Noah Peterson telephoned me half an
hour after Pixie had left. 'I am wounded, deeply
wounded.'

'Oh, er, good afternoon, Mr—er, Noah.' I knew
immediately what had happened. Pixie—blast her—had
trotted over to Noah Peterson in the guise of peacemaker
and promptly blown the gaff.

'Here I thought we had embarked upon a friendship—'
his voice throbbed with accusation—'and now I learn that
you still harbour the basest of suspicions about me.'

'Er . . .' There was not much I could say to that—not to
him. I would have plenty to say to Pixie when I saw her
again.

'I can assure you, Rosemary, I was nowhere near your
premises last night. I was otherwise engaged—very
engaged. Pitti-Sing was having her kittens. She had a
difficult time, poor darling. I was up all night with her.
So was the vet.'

'Congratulations,' I said quickly. 'How many did she
have? I'll bet they're darling.'

'She had three—the first litter is often small. But they're beautiful,' his voice softened and became lyrical. 'Exquisite, enchanting—I can almost forgive Errol. Certainly I wish him no harm.'

'I'm delighted to hear it.'

'Then prove it to me. Prove that we're really friends—and help me to celebrate. Let me take you—and the children—to dinner again tonight at Gino's Place.'

'But what about Pitti-Sing? If she's just had her kittens, surely you don't want to leave her alone.'

'Of course not. Pixie Toller has volunteered to sit with her for the evening. In fact, she suggested it. So that we could bury the hatchet, as it were. Properly, this time. She's quite right, I'm most grateful to her.'

'I see.' I saw far more than Noah realized. By throwing me to the wolves, Pixie had arranged it so that she could have the Peterson house—and the Sacred Ground—to herself tonight. Oh, she'd look after Pitti-Sing, all right, probably between Rain Dances.

'Don't be annoyed,' Noah said anxiously. 'I've been wanting to invite you out again. I didn't have to be pushed into it. Please say you'll come, all of you.'

It would serve Pixie right if I refused. That would teach her to try to involve innocent bystanders in her hare-brained schemes. Momentarily I pictured Noah, having settled down to a quiet evening with Pitti-Sing and the new kittens, being disturbed by whatever drumbeats or war whoops Pixie might consider part of the ceremony and going out to discover her in full Rain Dance. I wondered if she had devised a suitable costume for the ritual.

'You still don't trust me,' he said. 'Even when I have an alibi that proves I'm innocent.'

'Don't be silly. Of course, I trust you.' *Did I?* At least, I believed he hadn't been stalking Errol last night. 'I simply

made a light remark to Pixie and she exaggerated it out of
all proportion.'

'She often does,' he agreed. 'But there's usually a grain
of truth in what she says, just the same. She thinks it's
important that neighbours should be friends—and so do
I. Especially when there's danger threatening, as now,
and we might all have to depend on each other. So, why
not have a pleasant evening first—while there's still time?'

'Oh, all right.' I could not betray Pixie—even though
she had it coming. 'I mean, thank you, we'll be happy to
join you for dinner.'

'Wonderful! I'll pick you up about seven.'

I had hardly replaced the receiver when the phone rang
again. This time it was Celia.

'I've been thinking,' she said. 'If you're not feeling well,
you won't want to bother about a meal tonight. Why
don't we take the kids and eat at Gino's Place?'

'I can't,' I said. 'I mean, not with you. I've already
accepted an invitation from Noah Peterson. We'll see you
there. Perhaps we can join forces.'

'Oh—' Celia sounded rather strange. 'No, I don't think
so. Perhaps I won't go. I don't mind cooking tonight. I
was thinking of you.'

She was thinking of something else, too. I recognized
the note in her voice. She wasn't—she couldn't—be
thinking of matchmaking, could she? Not so soon.

'Celia,' I said warningly. 'Celia, I assure you. Whatever
you're thinking, you're wrong. Noah Peterson only wants
to be neighbourly. The children are coming and—'

'Rosemary!' Celia sounded genuinely shocked. 'How
could you think I'd think such a thing? I know what you
and John meant to each other. I may not say much about
it, but I know—' her voice broke. 'I know how you must
be feeling.'

'I'm sorry.' Of course she knew. She was next for the

high jump. Furthermore, she had been forewarned. She must have given it a lot of thought.

'Look.' Her voice was bright, too bright, now. 'Since you're all fixed up for tonight, let's plan something nice we can do later in the week. All of us. I know—let's drive over to the coast and go on that Whale Watch! How about tomorrow—or the next day? I'll ring and make reservations.'

'That sounds like fun.' Tessa and Timothy would love it. 'Why don't we make it next week, though? I—'

'No!' Her voice rose unsteadily. 'The sooner the better. Let's have a few laughs while we're able to. Patrick—' she broke off.

Had Patrick taken a turn for the worse? Celia was haunted by something more than she was going to admit, although she had just come very close. I waited, but she didn't say anything more.

'All right,' I said. 'We'll do it this week.'

'Tomorrow?' She asked gratefully. 'Please, Rosemary, tomorrow?'

'All right,' I agreed. 'Tomorrow.'

CHAPTER 16

It looked as though half the town—the more affluent half—had decided to dine at Gino's Place that night. Viv and Hank Singleton greeted us effusively as we passed their table. I was rather less effusive. When I had been at Celia's the other day, I could not help noticing that the Victorian tea-trolley and the silver-topped claret jug had disappeared. It was not the Singletons' fault that Celia had to sell them her cherished possessions, but it did not endear them to me.

Gino led us to a table by a window at one side of the

room and whipped away a RESERVED notice.

'You kids sit here—' Noah directed. 'I ordered this table especially,' he murmured to me while the children were seating themselves. 'You can't see the lobster tank from here. I know it upset you folks last time.'

'That's very kind of you.' It would not be kind of me to cavil that I could see the kitchen door from my seat and would thus still be aware of the struggling victims being borne to their doom. Noah was trying very hard. I smiled at him and edged my chair round so that I had an alternative view out of the window on to the little square across the street.

'Look, Mummy.' Timothy twisted round and waved to someone in the centre of the room. 'There's Dexter!'

'Is he out of bounds again?' Noah turned and frowned. 'No. He's got Greg with him.'

'Hi, Noah, Mrs Blake . . .' Dexter materialized beside our table. 'Gee, I'm glad to see some friendly faces.' He looked and sounded faintly desperate. 'I mean, I'm glad to see *you*—'

'What's the matter, Dexter?' Noah asked.

'Oh, nothing,' Dexter said unconvincingly. 'Not really. It's just—' He took a deep breath and blurted it all out:

'It's Greg. They got a report from the dentist this morning—so he's got to believe it. It *was* Lois. He was pretty upset. I got my allowance today, so I thought I'd take him to dinner and cheer him up. But it isn't working. I can't get through to him. He's just sitting there—' Dexter's voice cracked—'staring into space. When I say something, he doesn't answer. I don't know what to do.'

Poor Dexter. It was more than he could handle. He was learning the hard way that life was not the way it was presented on the television screen. When people were cruelly wounded, they did not leap up with a merry laugh after the commercial—they lay there and bled.

Sometimes they died.

And when a friend and partner died, they did not shrug it off with a brave tight-lipped smile and go out on the town and forget about it—they felt the pain. Sometimes they went into shock—deep shock.

Greg was sitting at a table for two, looking blankly at the empty chair across from him. The last time I had seen him at that table, Lois had been in that empty chair.

Noah and I met each other's eyes.

'Look, son,' Noah said gently. 'Why don't you and Greg come over here and join us?'

'Could we?' Dexter's shoulders straightened as though the weight of the world had just rolled off them. 'Look, I'll pay for us—for all of you. It will be my party. I've got plenty of money—'

'Don't you worry about that,' Noah said. 'You go and get Greg. The rest of us will push our chairs together. It will be a bit of a squeeze, but we'll manage.' He signalled to the waiter for two extra chairs.

Rudi disappeared behind the scenes and returned with the two chairs. He placed them solicitously, holding Greg's chair for him. Greg barely appeared to notice that we were there. He gave the ghost of a social smile and resumed staring into the distance.

'We're going on a whale watch tomorrow,' Timothy told Dexter.

'Hey, that's great. Some guys have all the luck.' Dexter was regaining his bounce now that he no longer felt solely responsible for Greg. 'Can I come, too? I'll pay my own way—'

'Haven't you just about used up your passes for this month?'

'Oh, that's okay. I can sneak out and meet—' Dexter broke off, abruptly recalling his silent companion. He glanced at Greg uneasily. Greg did not appear to have heard a word.

'You like to order now?' Rudi was back, flourishing his order pad. He bent over Dexter ingratiatingly. 'Steak Diane very good tonight. Maybe Steak Diane for everybody?'

'Uh, I don't think so.' Dexter was learning tact; he looked at Greg. 'No—not for me. I don't know about anybody else?'

'Definitely not,' I said. With Greg in the state he was in, it would be major cruelty to allow Rudi to go flaunting flames in front of him.

'Big mistake—' Rudi was beginning to sulk, sensing that he would not get the opportunity for his gala performance at this table. 'Steak Diane specially good tonight.'

'Not tonight,' Noah vetoed firmly.

'Crêpes Suzette, maybe, for dessert?' Rudi was not going to give up without a struggle. 'Crêpes Suzette ver' good tonight.'

'I'd rather have ice cream,' Tessa said. Her sidelong glance at Greg betrayed that she was being tactful, too.

'I should think we'd all have ice cream.' Noah disappointed Rudi again.

'Big mistake,' Rudi muttered, dying hard. He shrugged and waited for our orders as though he had lost all interest in whatever we were going to have.

We ordered and I looked around the restaurant. It was apparent that Rudi was getting no chance to show off tonight. It was unrealistic of him to expect it. Surely he must realize that, with the fire in the woods endangering the town, no one was going to want to be reminded of it.

'Are you all right, Greg?' Timothy asked uncertainly. Noah and I exchanged glances. It was the question we had not quite dared to ask.

'Oh, yeah, sure, Tim,' Greg answered mechanically. He was still a million miles away.

'Greg—' Impulsively I put my hand over his. 'I'm so

sorry about Lois.'

'It *was* her. It couldn't have been, but it was.' He turned to me, shaking his head. 'I can't understand it. What was she doing way out there? She told me she was coming into town. Why should she lie to me?'

'Perhaps she didn't.' The more I thought about it, the more certain I was that I was right. 'Perhaps she *did* come into town, to meet someone. He may have strangled her here and then taken her body to the shelter—'

Something cold and wet and red as blood splashed over our hands. I shrieked and jumped.

' 'Scusi, madame, 'scusi—' Rudi mopped feverishly at my hand with a napkin. 'The tomato juice spill. Ver' sorry. An accident. 'Scusi.'

'It's all right.' I removed my hand from his frantic ministrations. He shifted his attention to Greg and dabbed at his hand.

'You're right.' For the first time, Greg was looking at me as though he saw me. 'That must have been what happened. Lois wouldn't have lied to me.'

Another couple came in and took the table Greg and Dexter had vacated. Rudi muttered something in his own language—it could have been a curse or an expression of relief and deserted us to rush over and bring menus to the new people. Almost immediately, he seemed to be in dispute with them. It would appear that they did not wish to order the Steak Diane either.

'What's the matter with Rudi?' Noah wondered. 'He seems to be building up quite a head of steam tonight.'

'He's temperamental.' Dexter spoke with the voice of experience. 'He's having a fit because he can't play his big scene—like some ham actor who's just had his best lines cut.' Momentarily, disconcertingly, Dexter's face became faintly Latin, his eyes flashed, his upper lip curled back; he was Rudi about to throw a scene—or a knife.

'He is in a bad mood—' Gino spoke behind us. 'It was

necessary for me to have words with him this morning. He is not working out well. I apologize for my cousin. He will improve—or he will leave, I assure you.'

'We're all on edge these days,' Noah said soothingly.

'With reason,' Gino sighed. 'With good reason.' He bent over Greg. 'My friend, I am so sorry. There is nothing one can say . . . can do . . .' He patted Greg's shoulder ineffectually.

'I am sending over brandies—on the house,' he informed Noah.

'That's very kind—' But Gino was gone, following his cousin into the kitchen. We heard raised voices.

'She came to meet someone . . .' Greg had been oblivious of everything, following the painful trail of his own thoughts. 'Someone in this town—' His gaze ranged searchingly across the tables. 'I'll find out who. And when I do—' His hands clenched convulsively.

'Take it easy, fella,' Noah said. 'That's for the police to investigate. Chief Rogers—'

Greg said something totally out of character about Chief Rogers and didn't even apologize. He seemed to have forgotten there were children at the table and that he was supposed to set a good example. Some parents would have removed their children from Camp Mohigonquin immediately if they could have heard him.

'Steady on—' I said automatically, glancing at the children. Tessa was being a proper little lady and giving no indication that she had heard the last remarks at all. Timothy was struggling to keep a straight face. Dexter was unconcerned; he had heard far worse on visits to his parents.

Rudi brought our orders, dealing them off the tray as though he were riffling out cards from the bottom of the deck. His face was thunderous. He didn't really care whether we got the right orders or not.

Tessa and Timothy quietly swapped plates. Greg stared

at his indifferently until Noah reached over and exchanged it with mine. Even then, he continued to stared at it blankly.

'Come on,' Noah said. 'You've got to eat something. Keep up your strength.'

'Yeah, sure.' Greg picked up a fork and began pushing the food around his plate mechanically.

'I hope you don't mind,' Noah said, 'but if you're not going to eat all those scallops, could I have them for my kitty-bag? Pitti-Sing is eating for four now.'

'And we'll have Dexter's leftovers for Errol,' Tessa said stoutly, before the belated realization struck her that Dexter was highly unlikely to leave anything on his plate.

'Yeah, sure.' Greg looked around vaguely, as though ready to tip everything into a kitty-bag there and then. 'I'm not very hungry, I guess. Sorry, Dexter.'

'Aw, that's okay.' The lineaments of Dexter's face shifted subtly to mirror the devastation underlying Greg's expression.

'You're going to be an awfully good actor someday, Dexter,' I said. 'You're going to outdo everyone in your family.'

'Me?' he squeaked, gratified and incredulous.

'You,' I predicted firmly. 'You're going to be the finest Herbert of them all.'

'Well, gee—' His ears turned red, he shrank back against his chair. He was accustomed to complaints and disapproval; he had never learned to deal with compliments. He would. 'Well, thanks . . .' He swallowed and smily shyly. 'Thanks a lot.'

'I'll kill him!' Greg exploded suddenly. 'Whoever killed Lois—I'll find him and, with my bare hands, I'll kill him!' He shoved his plate away and lifted his head, glaring wildly around the room.

Hank Singleton intercepted Greg's gaze, winced, and raised his hand to signal for his bill.

'Greg—' I tried to calm him. 'You're frightening people. You'll empty the restaurant—'

'I don't care!' He glared with renewed fury. People at the adjoining tables began to edge their chairs away.

Now Viv had joined Hank in trying to catch their waiter's eye. It could be the beginning of a mass exodus if we couldn't get Greg under control.

Unfortunately for them, the customers were too conventional to leave without paying their bills—and they could not pay them unless they got them.

Rudi was paying no attention to his tables. He had withdrawn to lounge against the wall by the swing doors leading into the kitchen. He was in a monumental sulk. brooding over his unrequired trolley. At some point, he must have lit the spirit lamp; now he kept playing with it, turning the flame up, lowering it, then turning up to full force again. He was totally preoccupied; a child with a toy. A dangerous toy . . . a dangerous child—no, man, which made him even more dangerous. The leaping flame cast shadows, masking and unmasking the brooding face. The reflection of the flame glinted in his eyes, turning him into a stranger—a mad stranger.

'What's the matter, Rosemary?' Noah asked softly. I was aware that the others took one look at my face and then turned to see what had caused my expression.

They sat rooted for a moment watching the spectacle: Rudi, completely off guard and unaware of anything except the bright beckoning flame. Rudi, playing with fire.

Rudi—the pyromaniac! I remembered the look on Lois's face the last time we dined at Gino's. She had watched the Steak Diane ceremony and there had been sudden comprehension—and fear—in her face. But she was young, modern and liberal. She would not report anyone on mere suspicion. Possibly she was not sure of her diagnosis. She would want to give him the benefit of the doubt. So she had agreed to meet him—perhaps to discover if he had an alibi for the times when the fires were started; perhaps to urge him to seek psychiatric treatment. Whatever the reason, that meeting had sealed her fate.

'It's him!' Greg lurched to his feet. 'I'm going to kill the Christ-forsaken son-of-a-bitch!' he howled, starting forward, before we could catch him.

Then everything seemed to happen at once.

Rudi looked up and saw Greg rushing at him. With a wordless howl of his own, he tipped over the spirit lamp and spilled brandy and butter into the flames. He kicked the blazing trolley in the direction of our table before diving through the swing door into the kitchen.

The blazing trolley hurtled towards our table. With a violent oath, Noah leaped to his feet and kicked out at it as it rolled close. It rocked, tottered—spilling some of the flaming oils on to the floor, then reversed and headed off in another direction.

Screaming, the diners leaped up and scattered.

I sat frozen, with an unimpeded view of the kitchen door, and knew that worse was still to come.

There were shouts and screams from beyond the swing door, oaths and crashings of crockery. There was a violent hissing and muffled explosion. Then a blazing stream of vegetable oils cascaded under the door and out into the dining-room.

'No! No!' I screamed as people helpfully tilted the water carafes from their tables on to the flaming mess. The oil-based flames leaped and rode on top of the water into the heart of the dining-room, catching at the hanging table-cloths, setting them alight.

'I'll kill him!' Greg shouted, charging through the flames towards the kitchen door.

There was pandemonium in the restaurant as people jumped up and collided rushing for the exits, the flames licking at their trouser legs and skirts.

'No!' I heard myself sobbing. 'No! No!' I reached out for my children and, as in a nightmare, found Dexter clinging trustingly to me.

'This way!' Noah shouted. He had Tessa in his arms, Timothy holding to his coat-tail. He kicked out the window beside us and jumped through, hurling Tessa to the precarious safety of the little park. He disengaged Timothy and shoved him after Tessa, then stepped back into the blazing smoke-filled room for me.

'This way!' I felt my hand gripped tighter, I was propelled forward and tugged over the window-sill, Dexter still attached to me. We whirled through space and collapsed under the maples and pines with the children.

One-two . . . pause . . . *one-two* . . . The air was rent by the fire whistle signalling the most dreaded code of all: *the centre of town.* . . . *'One-two* . . . Sirens whooped and shrieked as the engines turned out to fight for Gino's Place.

'This way!' Noah kept shouting. 'This way!' I realized that he had stayed behind. He had taken up a post by the window and was pushing other patrons of the restaurant to safety.

'My God!' Hank and Viv Singleton stumbled across the street. The town square had become a gathering place for the refugees. 'My God—what happened?'

'The firebug—' I watched Noah anxiously. 'It was Rudi—the waiter.'

'The one who always wanted to do Steak Dianes,' Dexter said. 'Nobody would let him tonight, so he got mad—'

'And decided to barbecue the customers instead?' Viv stared in horror as a shower of sparks shot upwards from the roof. There was a sharp cracking sound as the front plate-glass window buckled and shattered.

'Noah!' I screamed.

'Greg!' Dexter shouted.

'We're okay—' Noah was beside us, Gino half-carried on his shoulders. 'I think we've got everybody out—as many as we could.'

'Greg—' Dexter said, staring at the blazing pyre of Gino's Place. 'What's happened to Greg?'

'Let's hope he got out the back door,' Noah said. 'Nobody could get through into the kitchen—it was an inferno in there.'

'It's not much better out here,' Hank said.

'No—' Mesmerized, we watched tongues of flame traverse the sloping roof of the kitchen annexe and entrench themselves in the eaves of the Gift Shop next door. Another shower of sparks flew into the sky and travelled outwards.

'Come on.' Hank caught Viv's arm as the fire engines rolled up. 'Let get to the shop and see what we can save. This town is going to go up like a tinder-box!'

Other people obviously thought the same. For every one who stayed watching the fire, two more slipped away to their cars. We tried to stare around and behind the flames, hoping to see Greg emerging in safety. But there was no safety anywhere.

One . . . two . . . three . . . four . . . The fire whistle blasted off again. *One . . . two . . . three . . . four . . .*

'Good God!—that's us!' Noah's fingers bit into my arm. 'That's our side of the Lake!' He released me and raced for his car. 'Pitti-Sing! She's out there all alone—with her kittens!'

'Errol!' Panting, Tessa and Timothy kept pace with him. 'Errol's all alone, too!'

Nominally, Pixie Toller was cat-sitting Pitti-Sing and her kittens, but I did not feel sure enough of that to remind Noah. If Pixie was in the middle of some complicated ritual dance on the lake shore, I knew only too well that the whole forest could be ablaze before she noticed anything amiss. Even then, she might still consider it simply the darkness before the dawn—or, in her case, the firestorm before the cloudburst.

'Greg—' Dexter hung back as I tried to pull him into the car. 'What about Greg?'

'We can't do anything about him right now!' Noah was developing a fine technique for hurling people about. Dexter went tumbling into the back seat.

'The firemen will take care of Greg,' Noah promised unconvincingly.

CHAPTER 17

As we hurtled through the night the noise of whistles and sirens died away. The woods were uniformly dark and private with no pinpricks of light to disturb them; even the fireflies seemed to have gone to ground. We might have been in another, more peaceful, world; but danger was still all around us, seen or unseen.

'I'll drop you at your house,' Noah said, 'and go on and collect Pitti-Sing and the kittens. Then I'll come back for you. Be ready.' In the intermittent light of the street lamps I saw his jaw tighten. 'If the fire in the woods and the town fire link up—' He broke off and concentrated on the sharp turn leading up to the lake.

We could be trapped. Mentally I finished the sentence for him. For the sake of the children, neither of us would voice the grim knowledge.

A low deep rumble sounded in the distance. We were all too jaundiced to pay any attention to it. We had heard it too frequently, trusted in it too often. It was just another snare and delusion. Reality was the pall of smoke overhanging the woods; the flames creeping through the town.

'Of course,' Noah said thoughtfully, 'we ought to have suspected Rudi.' Carefully he enumerated the points: 'The classic arsonist is foreign, unsettled, male . . . The trouble is, we've had so many home-grown insurance frauds perpetrated by businessmen on the verge of bankruptcy, we tend to overlook the obvious textbook cases these days.'

'If I could borrow your boat—the Harpers' boat—' Dexter shook my shoulder, reclaiming my attention—'I could row across the lake and let Benjie know what's happened. Then we could get Camp Mohigonquin to safety.'

'Never mind the heroics,' Noah said grimly. 'You're staying with us. A telephone call will do to alert the camp. The lines aren't out yet.'

'Mummy,' Tessa said, 'Mummy, we'll get Errol out all right, won't we?'

'Of course we will,' I said definitely. 'And Pitti-Sing and her kittens, too.' That was all I was willing to guarantee but, with luck, the children wouldn't notice that.

'Here we are.' Noah drew up in front of the house. 'Get your things together and be waiting for me. I'll be right back.'

As we got out, I looked over my shoulder. Behind us, a red glow lit the sky. Even as I stood there, the Fire Alarm blasted its urgent message once again, with the added blast that meant it was calling in reinforcement from the neighbouring towns. Edgemarsh Lake needed all the help it could get.

'Hurry, Mummy—' Tessa tugged at my hand, dancing with impatience. 'Let's go and get Errol.'

'You telephone the Camp,' I directed Dexter as I unlocked the door. 'Then I'll ring Celia and tell her what's happened. She knew we were eating at Gino's, she'll have started worrying when she heard the town code.'

'I'll get our cases, Mummy.' Timothy dashed upstairs.

'Eeerr-rroll . . .' Tessa called. 'Eeerr-rroll . . .' She raced for the kitchen.

'What can I do, Mrs Blake?' Dexter asked, putting down the telephone. Now that he had alerted the camp, he seemed lost and momentarily bewildered. 'Can't I do something to help?'

'Help Tim with the cases—' I took possession of the phone. 'You might look around upstairs and see if there's anything that fits you. You'll need something for overnight, at least. Look in Mr Harper's wardrobe—' None of Timothy's things would fit him. 'No—' I remembered that all the Harper family clothing was stored in the basement room. But there was Celia's Boston shopping—she hadn't retrieved it yet. 'Look in the cupboard in the front bedroom—in the carrier bags from the Boston stores. There might be something in one of them you could wear, at a pinch.'

'And this is a pinch!' he agreed, darting for the stairs.

'Mummy—' Tessa returned, tearful. 'Mummy, I can't find Errol anywhere. He isn't here. He's got out—'

'He couldn't have. Shh—just a minute, Tessa, then I'll help you look. Hello—'

'Hello—' It was Luke, sounding sleepy and faintly puzzled. No, I couldn't speak to Celia, or even Patrick—his parents weren't there. 'I thought they were with you, Aunt Rosemary. I'm sure they were going to have dinner with you.'

'Those plans were changed. They're not here.' Where could they be? And what was to be done about Luke, alone in the house with the fire spreading towards him? Should we try to get over to collect him, or were Celia and Patrick on their way home even now? If they returned to find Luke gone and wasted valuable time searching for him, they might be trapped themselves.

In the sudden silence, as I tried desperately to decide what was to be done, there came the familiar hollow thud—the sound of a coffin lid falling. An omen? It couldn't be—it was real. And somewhere nearby.

'Errol!' Tessa burst into sobs, putting her own interpretation on the sound. 'Mummy, that man has shot Errol!'

'Don't be silly, darling. He has far more important things on his mind right now.' So had we all. 'Luke, listen—stay where you are. We'll either call back with instructions or come and get you. If your parents get back, ring through and let me know. If there's no answer, you'll know we're on our way.' It was the best I could do. Noah might have a better idea when he returned.

'*Prr-yah?*' Belatedly, Errol decided to respond to his name. Blinking sleepily, he crawled out from under the sofa and looked around inquiringly.

'There's Errol!' Tessa pounced on him, clutching him to her, Immediately he began to struggle to regain his freedom, yowling a protest.

Oh no—he was going to be difficult!

'Stay with me, Errol,' Tessa screamed. 'Mummy, I can't hold him! He's going to run away and be burned!'

'No, he isn't,' I said, thinking frantically. I had looked everywhere for Errol's carrying case without success. I could not believe he didn't have one. The only place I hadn't looked was in the Bluebeard's Room in the basement. Furthermore, I might be able to save some of the more portable treasures Nancy had stored down there. If I couldn't identify the sentimental treasures, at least I could salvage the most valuable.

I shook the bunch of keys, singling out the one I had never used. There was no spot of blood on it, but it was brighter and shinier than the others—as though it had never been used, or had recently been duplicated from an original. I started for the cellar stairs.

'*Ta-taa-ta-taa*—' The horn sounded out front, along with a more sedate honk, as two vehicles drew up. I heard car doors slam and went to the front door to meet them.

Rosemary—' Pixie rushed into the house. She was wearing a suede shift liberally bedecked with wampum beads. There were moccasins on her feet and a feathered headdress on her head, her face was resplendent with full war paint. I hadn't seen such colours and designs since the last time I had walked down King's Road. 'Rosemary, are you ready? Let's get out of here while the getting's good!'

'We've got to go and collect Luke,' I told her. 'Celia and Patrick have gone off somewhere—he's all alone in the house.'

'We can manage that.' Noah was immediately behind Pixie. His face was decorated by nothing more than a bemused expression, but it was enough. At some later moment I must get him to tell me his side of the story. 'There isn't that much rush. I checked with the Park Rangers at the lookout tower. The fire is breaking out of the containment area, but it hasn't reached the All-State Alarm stage yet.'

'Oh, good,' I said. 'I'm going down to Nancy's storeroom to try to find Errol's carrying case. If you'll come with me, Pixie, perhaps you can tell me if there's anything special down there Nancy would like me to save.'

'Sure thing.' Pixie followed me into the cellar, so did Noah. The children trailed along behind us, unwilling to let us out of their sight. Fortunately Errol had calmed a bit and was quiet in Tessa's arms—but he couldn't be depended upon to stay that way.

'Oh—*tchach!*' Pixie made an impatient exclamation as we walked through the playroom. 'Rosemary, do you mean to say—' she detoured over to the shadowy steps—'you've been leaving the bulkhead door unlatched?'

'I don't know,' I said honestly. 'Is it? I haven't noticed. We never use it.'

'That could be dangerous!' Pixie mounted the steps half way, bending over, then straightened and pushed the doors upwards to demonstrate. They moved easily at her touch.

'You see,' she scolded. 'They weren't locked.' She ducked again and let the doors fall shut. They fell smoothly and in perfect unison, making a small hollow thud—like the sound of a coffin lid falling.

'This house has been wide open—' Pixie reached up and slid home a large iron bolt. 'Anyone could have got in here any time they wanted. You're just lucky that crazy Rudi didn't decide to sneak in and start one of his fires here.'

'He'd have to know about it first,' I said weakly. The implications were more than I could face at this moment. I had to concentrate on the present danger. Somewhat unsteadily, I walked over to the storeroom.

I inserted the key in the lock, it turned easily. Nancy had obviously oiled it before her departure. Suddenly conscious of everyone behind me, I made a feeble joke:

'I declare this bazaar open—' I intoned, throwing wide the door. Pixie snapped on the lights and we moved forward into the room.

I almost tripped over a Victorian rosewood tea-trolley.

'There's Errol's carrying case!' Tessa's sharp eyes spotted it in a far corner of the room. She dashed to get it.

I stood rooted, spotting other things. A Chinese Chippendale mirror leaned against one wall. A Landseer stag-at-bay dominated a corner. A carriage clock and a silver-topped claret jug stood atop a Pembroke table . . .

Oh, there were lots of items I didn't recognize—

presumably Nancy's. But the others . . . What were they doing here? How had they got here?

'That's Nancy's mother—' For an insane moment, I thought Pixie was heading for the stag-at-bay, but she veered off and pulled a Forties' pastel from beneath the Pembroke table. She straighted with it and looked around in some confusion.

'And that's Arnold's Do-It-Yourself tool kit,' she identified. 'But it would be a favour to Nancy if you let that get burned up. She'd want her grandmother's ivory manicure box—it's going to go to Donna someday, but—' Pixie frowned. 'It's strange. There's a lot of stuff here that's not Nancy's. It seems vaguely familiar—but I can't quite place it.'

It did not seem the moment to tell her that I could.

'Errol's all right,' Tessa said with satisfaction. She had unceremoniously dumped Errol into his carrying case; he was wailing protest and grievance. 'We can go now.'

'Yes . . .' I agreed blankly.

'Don't worry,' Pixie said comfortingly. 'Even if the fire reaches the house and demolishes it, the cellar ought to be all right. They used to be called storm cellars, you know—because you could ride out a hurricane or a cyclone down here, no matter what happened to the rest of the house. You can probably leave everything here and it will be quite safe.'

'Probably—' Noah had been prowling the farther reaches of the room— 'but I wouldn't like to bet on it.' He paused by a large packing crate and inquired of it politely, 'Would you, Mrs Meadows?'

'Oh, *there* you are, Rosemary!' Celia emerged from behind the packing crate quite as though she had been expecting to find me there. Only a note of hysteria in her voice belied the attempted social tone. 'Patrick—here's Rosemary!'

'Oh, uh—' Patrick crept out from behind the matching

packing crate. 'Hello, Rosemary. We've been looking
everywhere for you.'

'Try again,' Noah suggested drily. 'That one doesn't
quite hold water.'

'Celia—Patrick—' Pixie was agog. 'What are *you* doing
down here?' She looked again at some of the semi-familiar
objects, this time placing them in context. 'Oh . . .' she
said, then abruptly enlightened, '*Ooohh!*'

'I'd suggest we leave now,' Noah said, 'and sort this out
later. Pitti-Sing and her kittens are waiting for me in the
car and she'll be getting worried if I'm not back pretty
smartly.'

Rebuked, we followed him upstairs. Dexter and
Timothy brought up the rear with much whispering,
nudging and snickering. They were taking an inordinate
interest in Celia and Patrick.

'I don't understand,' Celia said. 'Why have you come
back so early? And what were you all doing in the
storeroom?'

It seemed that we might more fairly ask that question,
but Noah countered with a different question:

'Didn't you hear the Fire Whistle? The second one—for
the North woods?'

'We've been busy,' Celia said primly. Then the full
import of the question struck her. 'The North? Oh no! We
just heard the signal for the town— No!'

We stepped out on to the porch, the sky red above us.
A great rolling explosion echoed in the distance.

'That's it!' Pixie said. 'They've begun dynamiting the
fire-break.'

Something pattered like shrapnel on the roof of the
porch. I hoped it was just stones and dirt—not burning
pine cones.

'Luke—' Celia said desperately. 'Luke—'

'We'll get him,' Patrick said. 'He'll be all right.'

'The house is going to burn down—' Celia began to

laugh hysterically. 'It's going to burn anyway!'

'Celia—' Patrick said warningly.

We went down the steps, down the path. Stones were pattering all around us.

'Ow!' Tessa complained. 'They hurt, Mummy.' She was still carrying Errol's case and could not protect her face adequately.

'Here—give me Errol—' Even as I took over the case, I became aware of a strangeness about the stones: they were all white; they bounced as they hit the ground; when they finally settled, they perched uneasily, then began to melt.

The deep rolling sound came again, climaxed by a great crash; the landscape sprang into bright relief. Large gobbets of water began to mix with the stones.

'It's hail!' Pixie halted and turned her paint-streaked face upwards. 'It's raining and hailing! It worked!'

'Rain!' Celia cried. 'Rain!'

The rain was gathering force. The parched earth could not drink it in immediately. Pools of water formed at our feet; rivulets followed the slope of the land.

'Thank God,' Noah breathed.

We stood there, faces upturned, glorying in the gorgeous soaking downpour. The hail disappeared but the rain continued, settling in for the night. Already the red glow in the sky was lessening.

'It's raining—really raining!' Celia was sobbing with relief. 'You can't do it now—it's too late!'

'Celia!' Patrick caught her by the shoulders and began shaking her.

'It's too late,' Celia insisted thankfully. 'The house is saved. It's not just the rain, Patrick—we've been rumbled!'

CHAPTER 18

We met at the entrance of the hospital. Pixie, Gino and I had just donated our pints of blood; Celia, Patrick and Noah were on their way in to donate theirs.

'How is he?' Noah asked.

'Holding his own.' Pixie reported what we had been told. 'Greg's pretty tough. He'll pull through.' She glanced at Gino and said hastily, 'Of course, it's too bad—'

'It is better that Rudi died,' Gino said heavily. 'Better he should have died before he ever come to this country—before he was born, even. I am shamed that my cousin—'

'It wasn't your fault,' Noah said quickly. 'How were you to know?'

'His family were too eager to send him to me—I should have suspected something wrong. Instead, I thought it was just ambition. It offered so much for him, if he had been the right sort. A partnership eventually, at least. Instead, I have lost my restaurant and must start over. If people will still come to a Gino's Place after what I have done to the town.'

'You just go ahead and rebuild,' Pixie said comfortingly. 'We'll all come back. Nobody is responsible for what their relatives do—thank heavens!'

Amen to that. I carefully refrained from looking at my would-be fraudulent sibling and her husband. In the post-mortems after their discovery, they had admitted planning the desperate gamble to pay off their debts and regain solvency. For months, they had been denuding their home of its most valuable contents, while leaving them on the household inventory held by the insurance company. At first, they had simply sold them to the Singletons. Later, when I had agreed to occupy the Harper residence, they had planned to secrete Celia's most prized antiques in the storeroom. Celia had duplicated the key before handing it on to me; she had also unbolted the bulkhead door so that Patrick could gain access to the cellar without my knowledge. What a shock I had given him when I opened the guest room window the other night and leaned out. They had not known that I had changed from the master bedroom at the front to the cheerful little guest room overlooking the bulkhead. After that, had come Celia's pressing invitations, designed to get me away from the house so that Patrick could make the last trips with the remainder of the antiques, before firing their house while it could be blamed on sparks from the blaze in the North woods.

At least, I tried to look on the bright side, Celia had not lied to me completely. Patrick was ill—but not dying. It had been one last summer in her beloved home she had been pleading for when I overheard them.

'You are all very kind.' Gino smiled at Pixie and then at the rest of us. 'It is a pleasure to live here at Edgemarsh Lake with you. And now I must go for a consultation with the architect who will design the new Gino's.' He descended the steps and walked away slowly.

'Isn't it ironic?' Pixie looked after him. 'Gino's Place was the most successful business for miles around. He must have been just about the only person in town who didn't *need* to collect on his fire insur—' She broke off abruptly, glanced at Patrick and turned bright red.

Patrick and Celia retained their bright social smiles, showing no reaction to Pixie's gaffe. I looked at them curiously, wondering if there was anything else they knew that they were not telling me. There had been another frantic letter from Nancy in the morning post:

Dear Rosemary, she had written,

No matter what you might hear—don't worry. It just looks a lot worse than it really is. The builders tell me that it can all be put right very quickly—and it will never show when they've finished. It won't cost all that much, either. Naturally, we'll pay for it our-selves, although I think Lania ought to contribute something, if not half. After all, her kids did their share of the damage. But we'll work that out between ourselves—it has nothing to do with you.

The good news is that Esmond has begun to feel totally comfortable with us. For the first time yesterday, the darling leaped up on the kitchen table and stole a lamb chop! I'm so happy that he has accepted us at last.

The workmen are at the door, so must close now. Don't worry about anything. By the time you get back, you'll never be able to see that it happened.

Kisses to Errol—

Nancy.

Don't worry. My home had been in one piece when I left it. My cat had never been a thief. What was it all about? Had she also written to Patrick, confiding in him?

Patrick looked back at me with a guileless smile. Now that his scheme had been thwarted, both he and Celia were looking more relaxed—and years younger. Celia was talking about finding a job and they were both due for a talk with their Bank Manager later in the week. It would take time, but they would sort out their finances in a more socially responsible manner.

'If you'd care to hang around for about half an hour,' Noah said to me, 'I can give you a lift back.'

'Thank you,' I said, 'but I've grown braver. I'm using the Harpers' car now.' It was silly not to use transport when I had it available. Just as it was silly to worry about road accidents when worse could befall you through no fault of your own when you were quietly going about your own business at home.

'Fine,' he said. 'I'm glad to hear it.' He did not look particularly delighted.

'Pixie is coming to dinner tonight,' I said. 'Why don't you come along, too? I'm not a bad cook and it's about time I began to repay some of the hospitality I've been receiving.'

'I'd like that.' This time he did look pleased. 'Thank you.'

'Don't forget,' Celia said. 'We're still going on that whale watch. Next week.' There was a lilt in her voice. She could look forward to it now, knowing that her home would still be standing when she returned from the expedition. This time it would be a pleasure trip—not an alibi.

'Fine,' I said.

'And we're taking a trip or two across the border before you leave,' Pixie reminded me. 'It's silly to be so near to Canada and not visit Montreal and Quebec—they're such beautiful cities.'

'Fine,' I said again. A sad detached feeling began slipping over me. John had planned sorties across the Canadian Border, too. We had been so thrilled and excited about it.

I said my goodbyes and walked down the steps slowly and turned towards the car.

At the foot of the steps, I stopped and lifted my face to the cool rain-washed breeze. The scent of wet ashes still hung in the air, but it was fading. Over towards the lake, the sky was dotted with dark glorious rain clouds. It was a beautiful day in a beautiful country.

Perhaps, some day, I would discover what one did in Illyria.

THE END